M000297464

The Birthday

CONFIDENT THAT SHE was the dominant member of her family, and the one to whom the others were bound by ties of love and loyalty, Meriel Graham expected that on her birthday it would, as usual, be everyone's concern to give her pleasure. However, under the normal surface of the day, all were occupied with problems of their own, so that the anniversary was remembered only by accident.

At the end of the day's surprises, faced with revelations which, if acknowledged, could result in the loss of her prized security, Meriel shrinks from self-recognition. It is Peter, her husband, who, after all the unhappiness her obtuseness has caused, is determined that in future she will not dictate the manner of their lives.

MARGARET YORKE

The Birthday

This title first published in the U.S.A. 1991 by
SEVERN HOUSE PUBLISHERS INC of
271 Madison Avenue, New York, NY 10016.
Originally published in Great Britain 1963 by Hurst & Blackett
Limited. This edition published in Great Britain 1991 by
SEVERN HOUSE PUBLISHERS LTD
of 35 Manor Road, Wallington, Surrey SM6 0BW

Copyright © Margaret Yorke 1963

British Library Cataloguing in Publication Data
Yorke, Margaret
  The birthday.
  I. Title
  823.914 [F]

  ISBN 0 – 7278 – 4165 – 3

Printed and bound in Great Britain
by Billing and Sons Ltd, Worcester

FOR
BOBBY AND LESLIE

*All the characters and events described in this
novel are imaginary.*

I

At seven, the house began to wake. One by one, its inmates surfaced from the releasing depths of sleep and acknowledged the new day. Outside, rain dripped from the surrounding trees and swelled the pools lying in hollows on the gravelled drive. The grass beyond, pierced with the last daffodils whose dejected heads drooped against the weather, shone wetly, shaggy with spring growth. A window at one end of the long building was briefly filled as a face peered out at the depressing prospect, to be soon withdrawn: Hanni, the Swiss maid, was stirring. Of necessity the first to rise, she was soon in the kitchen clattering pots and singing as she began to prepare breakfast.

In the largest bedroom, facing south-west, Peter Graham kept his eyes closed while he indulged in a further few seconds' respite. He had, as always, woken when Hanni riddled the boiler; the noise echoed along all the pipes in the house as she daily performed this chore before letting it draw; later, when he went downstairs himself, he raked it out and filled it. In a moment there would be the warning bell and sound of gushing liquid with which the electric Teasmade daily called the Grahams. Meriel would stretch and yawn before pouring out their two cupfuls; Peter would reach for his from the table between them, and Meriel would light her first cigarette. Morning would be admitted.

But today something was different, and he struggled, unwillingly fighting the inertia which made him long to submerge again, in an effort to recollect why. He looked warily at Meriel. She lay back against the pillows, calm, and still with much of the beauty he had found entrancing when she was young, her cigarette already lighted; she wore a mask of careful indifference, and just in time, before the façade cracked, he remembered that it was her birthday.

'Happy birthday, darling,' he greeted her, climbing out of bed with new energy in his relief at dredging up this fact, and pilgrimaging in his bare feet and striped pyjamas round the room to kiss her. She smiled at him, her eyes fine features in a soft face, and exhaled a cloud of smoke. Peter blinked and turned away, beginning the journey towards his dressing-room. 'You don't look thirty, let alone forty-two,' he said with hearty gallantry. 'I'm afraid you're going to have to wait for your present till this evening. It wasn't ready yesterday and I'm collecting it today.'

He opened the door and passed through, closing it behind him, then leaned against it for a moment hoping his invention had sounded convincing. He'd so nearly forgotten altogether.

Meriel continued to smoke, and drink her tea. She reclined in frills of lace, relaxed and perfectly content. How like Peter to be giving her something so special that it required preparation; not for him the hasty bunch of flowers and cheque offered by some husbands. Images of monogrammed cigarette cases and engraved pieces of jewellery swam before her mind's eye. She continued to smile.

Meriel was a completely happy woman. All her life she had only had to acknowledge a whim for it at once to be satisfied; the only girl, youngest in a family of five, she had been petted and indulged as a child by her parents and her brothers. She grew up to accept homage as her due, and later her fresh beauty and the poise she gained from innate confidence ensured her a constant band of admirers, from among whom she chose to marry Peter. Sometimes she wondered why she had selected him rather than any other; he had no particular claim to distinction except an appealing shyness; but on the whole she had no regrets. He had proved industrious and successful and was now the senior partner in an old-established firm of solicitors who dealt mainly with affairs of property. Although he ran no luxurious car at the expense of his business, like most of the men in the neighbourhood, but only a Morris Oxford paid for by himself, his income was a good one. Meriel herself had, when her parents died, inherited a comfortable fortune which guaranteed her independence and maintained the large estate-car which she used for the family. Besides this, Peter was both thrifty and generous. The Grahams had two children, neatly different as to sex; Meriel had produced them both with the minimum effort and discomfort, and her only cause for complaint was that Peter's absence abroad during the war had caused a wide gap between their ages. She herself had spent those years quietly, dully, but safely, in Devonshire with her parents, looking after the baby Caroline, and helping the local Women's Voluntary Services. She had been mildly bored, but she had extracted every ounce of satisfaction possible from maternity, growing plumper, softer, and more beautiful, while waiting with patience for Peter to return and resume his task of worshipping her. It never occurred to her that he might be altered in any way by his experiences. Though he received a slight wound in the leg, which still caused him to limp sometimes when he was tired, he had, as she calmly expected, returned seemingly unchanged apart from some lines round his eyes and, though she did not observe it, a mature strength about the mouth. Their life had since flowed pleasantly along, marked by the birth of Rupert, their removal from Kensington to Surrey, and finally, with increasing security, a further transition from Pilgrim's Cottage to Merelands.

And now it was her birthday. Her day.

Meriel rose slowly, put on her quilted dressing-gown and fluffy slippers, and prepared to greet it.

Rupert Graham had overslept. He was sprawled in his bed, with his straight dark hair falling across his forehead. A book lay face downwards on the floor beside him, where it had dropped from his hand when he fell asleep the night before. His bedside lamp still burned. Outside, the rain beat down and a branch of the climbing rose that covered this end of the house, loosened by strong winds from its detaining wire, tapped at the window; but Rupert slept on, and did not stir even when his mother, still in her dressing-gown, entered the room. She frowned as she picked up the book and read its title. It was a copy of *Hamlet*. Rupert's preoccupation with literature of all kinds caused her the only amount of genuine worry that she ever entertained. When left to himself he was always to be found sitting about 'with his nose in a book', as she called it, and that usually a volume of poetry. It was not hard to see why he slept so late, she thought, switching off his light and laying the book down with a little thud. Rupert did not move. Meriel gazed at him. His long, thin form and smooth face had a curiously defenceless appeal; he was still a child, and she still ruled over him. Though she might deplore his dreaminess and lack of practical sense, he was a nice-looking, well-mannered and obedient boy, and no doubt all this nonsense was simply a phase which he would outgrow. Meanwhile at least he spent much of his time in the holidays riding; that was a healthy occupation and one that prised him away from his books. She thought regretfully of how her own brothers had spent all the spare moments of their holidays in dashing from one violent physical activity to the next; they had seldom been known to read anything in those days. They had so far led exemplary lives, and were respectively a stockbroker, an insurance underwriter, a farmer and a company director. Certainly Rupert was like none of them; she fancied that in appearance he resembled her, and indeed his colouring was similar, but his thin, sensitive features were unique in the family. Peter could have told her that they were the replica of his own mother's when she was a girl, but obscurely he had felt it wiser not to disclose this information, and since his mother had died while Rupert was still a baby the likeness remained unobserved.

Suddenly, Rupert woke. He blinked, stretched, and was immediately alert. An expression of guilt came upon his face when he saw his mother bending over him, but it disappeared as he glanced quickly at the bedside lamp and saw that it was out.

Meriel missed the look, but she was intent on rebuke.

'Rupert, you're a naughty boy. You fell asleep over your book again,' she scolded. 'That's the fifth time these holidays. You can't be trusted, can you? I'll have to forbid reading altogether.'

'Sorry, Mum.' Rupert sat up and hugged his knees, his long forelock drooping into his eyes. He made himself look abashed.

'So I should think. Still, I'll let you off today,' she said, emphasising the last word.

Rupert wondered why.

'Thanks awfully,' he said warmly. 'I'll be down in a jiff. I am sorry, Mum,' he added earnestly, for good measure.

'Well, make sure it's the last time,' Meriel said. She left him then, and walked down the passage to the stairs. Her progress was regal. Meriel was tall and well-proportioned. As a girl she had been good at tennis, and still played a useful game. Now, as she prepared to descend the staircase, she automatically drew herself up and put back her shoulders; her carriage had always been good, and the thickening of her figure had only added dignity to her deportment. She went slowly down, and entered the dining-room.

The hatch leading into the kitchen was open, and Hanni's beaming face looked through.

'Good morning, Madame,' she called in her singing tones.

Meriel was always inordinately pleased by this respectful form of address which Hanni never failed to use and for which she was unique in the district.

'Many happy returns of the day,' Hanni continued. Her voice was very musical, as if a song lay behind the most mundane utterance. Rupert teased her and said it was years of yodelling that had made her speak this way.

'Thank you, Hanni,' said Meriel, walking over to the electric hot-plate and beginning to pour out her coffee. As she carried the full cup over to her place at the table, she saw that a small parcel wrapped in gaily striped paper waited by her plate. The sight of it drove Rupert's inexplicable defection in not greeting her from her mind; with pleased cries she unwrapped it, while Hanni, still framed in the hatch, watched happily. Soon a small bottle of toilet water was revealed.

'How lovely, Hanni, it is kind of you,' said Meriel. 'Just what I wanted. Thank you very much.'

'I hope you like the flavour,' said Hanni cheerfully. Her English was by now extremely fluent, but her choice of words was sometimes strange. Meriel and Peter had acquired her four years before during a holiday in her village; she had been with them ever since, apart from annual holidays when she returned, at their expense, to Switzerland. Meriel scarcely realised how fortunate they were in this arrangement. Things had always worked out for her, and she knew that if Hanni had not materialised, someone else would have appeared. She had never been without a 'mother's help' since Peter's return from the war, and in every case the description was no mere euphemism. Hanni was the latest in a successful series.

'Rupert overslept again,' Meriel said, now seated

and beginning to sip her coffee. 'He'd been reading late. He left his light on.'

'Ach, that one,' said Hanni indulgently. 'He'll wear out his eyes.' She made clicking sounds with her tongue. 'He's clever,' she added, and shook her head as if no good could come of this.

'He's tired,' Meriel said realistically.

'Well, he's growing,' said Hanni excusingly. She adored Rupert.

'Perhaps we could fit a time switch to his light,' said Meriel vaguely.

Hanni chuckled. 'The postman will be here soon,' she said. 'Lots for you today, I know.' She beamed again, and withdrew, closing the hatch. At once her voice, upraised in song, could be heard above the sound of water pouring into the sink as she began to wash up her own breakfast things and the saucepans.

Upstairs, Peter, now dressed in his dark suit, was in Rupert's room. He had entered as soon as he was sure Meriel was safely downstairs. Rupert, by this time out of bed, was at the window staring into the rain and wondering how, if you were a painter, you could possibly translate those globules of translucent grey into oils. Better, really, to work with words. He was surprised when his father came into the room, but not dismayed. He was not afraid of Peter.

'I overslept,' he volunteered at once.

'Reading late again?'

'Mm. I left the light on all night,' Rupert confessed. 'Sorry.' This time he spoke the truth. He hated offending his father, however trivial the reason.

'Hm. Well, try not to, there's a good chap,' said Peter. He was not really attending, intent on his mission. 'You know it's your mother's birthday, don't you? Hadn't forgotten, had you?'

A look of bafflement came and went across Rupert's expressive face.

'Hanni reminded me,' he said. 'And of course Mum was talking about it, you know how she does, to make sure we won't. She was in here just now, and I'd forgotten while I was asleep, so I didn't say anything. Hope she didn't mind. She was ticking me off about my light. I've got her a present.'

'Oh, good. That's all right, then.' Peter was relieved. He understood Rupert's reference to the way Meriel tended to refer to her birthday in the days before the event by relating everything to its distance from the date. Unfortunately, it seemed, he had not been listening attentively this year. 'It wouldn't do to forget. She'd be hurt,' he said now.

'Have you ever forgotten it?' asked Rupert curiously.

'Er—no,' said Peter, crossing his fingers.

'Golly, in twenty-two years! What a record,' exclaimed Rupert, impressed. He looked at his father with affectionate respect.

'Hurry up, old chap,' said Peter. 'Mother will be wondering where we are, and my train won't wait.'

Twenty-two years. The words echoed in Peter's brain as he went downstairs. What a long, long slice of life.

It did not take him long to finish the boiler's morning routine. Unlike most men, he did not regard himself as the only person gifted with the ability to understand its mysterious soul, but he thought stoking it an unsuitable task for Hanni, who anyway had enough to do already. Meriel would never have tackled it. During Peter's rare absences from home Hanni took over; she would have liked to do so daily, fearing always that Peter would get ash on his city suit, but at the same time she enjoyed the notion of humouring him. In fact, since the boiler was a modern installation, it was undemanding, and rarely dirtied its attendant.

Hanni beamed and sang on while he was in the kitchen, and only ceased her song when the postman arrived, tapping at the window as he passed from his van to the door. She exchanged a few words of badinage with him while she received a small pile of letters and parcels from his hands.

'For Madame, I expect,' she said gaily to Peter. 'She is happy on her birthday.'

Peter hoped this was a statement, not a pious wish.

'Thank you, Hanni,' he said, taking the mail from her and knowing very well that there were certain to be several dull business letters and bills for him among the communications. He began looking through them as he walked through the hall towards the dining-room.

'Mrs. Graham, Mrs. Graham, Mrs. Graham,' he intoned, dealing out a little heap in front of Meriel who was now finishing her second cigarette of the day. She began at once to open her parcels, as pleased and excited as a child and unaware that Peter was growing anxious as he scrutinised the writing of the last few addresses. His task ended, he went without speaking to the sideboard to pour out his coffee and help himself to bacon and eggs.

Meriel's first delight began to diminish when she had undone four parcels and discovered their contents to be soap, powder and bath salts, soap and bath cubes, hand cream, powder and bath salts, and finally powder and bath essence, in varied extremely expensive makes, the tributes of her brothers and their wives. Ruefully she held up Hanni's toilet water for Peter's notice.

He began to laugh. 'What a wealth of implication, Merry,' he said, but changed his attitude when he saw her crestfallen expression. She still felt like a child where her birthday was concerned.

'I suppose I could change some of them,' she said doubtfully.

'Give them back as presents next Christmas,' said Peter robustly. 'Anyway, my present isn't a bathroom one.'

'I hope not,' said Meriel pettishly.

Peter wondered what indeed it would prove to be; he lacked all inspiration. Now Rupert could be heard running noisily downstairs. He burst into the room, dressed in a red sweater and dirty brown corduroy trousers, looking hearty. He had not paused to brush his hair, and now hastily pushed the hanging lock back from his high forehead before greeting his mother.

'Hi, Mum,' he cried cheerily. 'Many happy returns of the day.' He leaned over Meriel and kissed her soundly on the cheek, meanwhile pressing a square parcel into the softness of her chest which she was resting on the table.

Meriel winced, retreating.

'Rupert darling, must you make so much noise?' she asked, beginning to tear off the paper.

Rupert became visibly deflated.

'Sorry,' he muttered, slouching over to fetch his own breakfast. A large glass of milk had already been put by Hanni at his place; she longed to fatten Rupert, and to this end poured milk into him and spent hours baking rich cakes and making apfelstrudel for his delectation. Rupert consumed all these offerings with appreciation but remained thin. He subsided into his chair and glanced at his father. Peter kept his own eyes resolutely turned towards his plate as he industriously arranged the last morsel of bacon on his fork. He was no longer hurt by Meriel's offhand lack of regard for mood, but he knew Rupert to be as vulnerable as once he had been himself.

Meriel began to open the box she had laid bare by the removal of the paper, and Rupert rallied, looking eagerly across the table in anticipation of her pleased reception of his gift. Verbena bath powder and soap tablets were revealed. Meriel's face went blank.

'I thought they'd go with that lotion stuff Hanni gave you,' Rupert began, and then his voice trailed away. For the first time he saw the other boxes, still open, littering the table among the yellow plates and cups. Anxiously he turned towards his father, and met his eye, full of pity not for him, but for Meriel, who now tried to pull herself together and express some gratitude.

'Lovely, Rupert. Think what a lot of nice baths I can have now,' she said.

'Poor Mum, it's too bad,' said Rupert, overcoming his own disappointment at the failure of his choice in a mature effort that did not escape his father's notice. 'You'll be cleaner than clean for ever, now. Never mind, I expect I can change mine, it only came from Boots. Perhaps you'd like one of those long brush things for getting at your back instead, like Aunt Sue has, they've got some there, shaped like fish. Or a sponge.' He spoke rapidly, acutely sensitive to his father's distress for Meriel but misinterpreting the reason. He tried a diversion. 'What's Caro sent?'

There was a silence, and Peter frowned repressively.

'Caroline seems to have missed the post,' said Meriel flatly.

'You'll hear from her this afternoon,' said Peter reassuringly. He should have written to remind the child, although she rarely forgot anniversaries. He'd ring her up when he got to the office. 'How are you going to spend the day?'

'Oh, I'm too old now to have a fuss made of my birthday,' said Meriel. Each year she voiced this opinion, but would have been aghast if her family had acted upon it. As far as possible, an atmosphere of fiesta was maintained throughout the day, and Peter made a supreme effort to catch an early train home. Neighbours came to lunch or drinks, and the Grahams dined out at an extremely expensive hotel ten miles away.

'I'm going to coffee at Edith's,' Meriel went on to inform her two men, more cheerfully. 'And Felicity's coming to lunch. Rupert will be out riding this morning, won't you, dear? So you'll be occupied.'

Rupert looked out of the window.

'It's raining hard,' he remarked.

'Martian needs exercise, wet or fine, and so do you,' his mother reminded him. 'You can't spend all day glued to a book. And if you're lucky enough to have a pony you must look after him, whatever the weather. Isn't it time he went to the blacksmith? You could take him this afternoon.'

'Yes, Mummy,' Rupert sighed. Peter looked at him sharply and recognised the defeat in his face. There was more to this than mere dislike of wet weather; he had known Rupert walk for hours on the common, coatless, in a deluge, and come home surprised at the dismay caused by his soaking condition. Here was something that must be sorted out, but not just now; it must wait.

'You'll be busy then,' he said to his wife.

'Yes, as usual. There's a meeting of the Drama Group this afternoon,' Meriel continued. 'We're casting the new play.'

In horrible embarrassment once yearly Peter was obliged to attend the annual production of the Timpsley Drama Group, whose members, mostly women, had too much time on their hands and needed a vehicle for self-expression and attracting attention. Lack of discernible talent held none of them back. Each play provoked a crop of feuds and misunderstandings among the cast; every year long-standing friendships were irreparably fractured while unlikely new alliances sprang into existence among the wreckage of wounded pride. A few people really enjoyed themselves, and one or two worked extremely hard in the interests of the rest.

'What's it going to be, Mum?' asked Rupert keenly, trying hard to restore the damaged atmosphere.

'*Candida*,' said Meriel. 'Shaw. And don't call me "Mum", please.'

'Sorry, Mum—I mean Mummy,' said Rupert, managing not to point out that he was well aware of who had written the play. He could not understand his mother's lack of sympathy with his own pursuit of reading when she indulged in ventures of this sort. He was too young to realise that she sought admiration and attention and did not mind where she went to look for it.

Peter knew this, however, and the knowledge made him feel guilty, as if throughout their life together he had consistently failed her, in spite of seizing every opportunity he saw of sparing her pain or giving her pleasure. His concern over her duplicated birthday presents was not just caused by her disappointment but rather by her childlike inability to move out of herself towards the giver; yet he did not blame her for this lack any more than he would have blamed a child.

'It should be good,' he said now, about the play, and looked at his watch. 'I must hurry or I'll miss the train. Goodbye, dear. I'll be on the five o'clock for sure.' I hope, he added mentally. Because it was her birthday he made a special effort over the post-breakfast, pre-departure kiss with which he daily parted from her, and tried to put into it more than the exasperated affection of habit which was all the feeling that nowadays Meriel could rouse in him. He did not notice Rupert watching them both with a power of shrewd observation that would have been remarkable in someone twice his age.

'I'll open the garage, Dad,' the boy said, thrusting back his chair and flinging down his table-napkin. He loped into the hall and out by way of the kitchen through the back-door to the yard. Peter followed, snatching his briefcase from the oak chest as he passed. Hanni held the door wide as father and son went through, Peter not so very much taller now than the boy, but stocky, a compact, muscular man. It was Hanni's hope that Rupert would eventually fill out and develop a similar sturdy build. She smiled as they went by, and rushed though he was, Peter still found time to say, 'Thanks, Hanni. Goodbye.'

He got into the car and started the engine while Rupert finished hauling back the heavy door that had warped a little on its runners. As he reversed out of the garage the boy came up to his window and bent down, his head close to his father's, anxious to prolong their period of communication.

'Pity about all that bath stuff,' he said. 'She minded.'

'These things happen,' Peter said, knowing suddenly that his son was very wise. He put the clutch out, his hand on the gear lever, then reached into the inner pocket of his jacket for his wallet.

'Nip down to Flynn's and get her some flowers,' he said, extracting two pounds and handing them to Rupert. 'In case Caro has forgotten—say they're from us all.'

Rupert stared at such a sum, but took it calmly.

'O.K. Shall I spend it all?' he asked casually.

'Oh yes—flowers cost the earth,' Peter told him,

slipping into gear and letting the car begin to move. 'Get a lot. Not daffodils—something that's out of season in the garden.'

'Carnations?' Rupert asked.

'Anything that looks nice, I leave it in your more than capable hands,' Peter said with a grin.

'What did you give her, Dad?' Peter asked, curiosity overcoming tact, running now beside the car as it proceeded to the gate.

'I'm picking it up in town today,' said Peter, thus disguising that he did not know the answer to this question. He changed up, and a plume of exhaust smoke puffed from the car as it moved out into the lane. Rupert waved after it, obscurely sorry to see it go, and his father, looking at him in the mirror, saw him turn and kick at the stones in the gateway before he ambled away with his hands in his pockets.

'Silly boy, he'll get wet through,' Peter thought, and spent the rest of the journey to the station wondering what he could buy that would give Meriel's birthday a happy ending, salve his own conscience, and create a good atmosphere for their traditional dinner. He was in the train unfolding *The Times* before he remembered Rupert's unexplained reluctance to ride his pony in the rain.

2

LEFT alone at the breakfast table, Meriel poured herself out a fresh cup of coffee, and lighted yet another cigarette, which she clamped firmly between her lips as she began sorting through her post again. She screwed up her eyes in an attempt to filter the smoke as she looked at her letters. She did not think it marvellous that all her brothers and their wives had remembered her birthday, for throughout her life this had always happened, but she was annoyed with Caroline; it was unlike her to be careless, but since she had been living in London it had been less easy for Meriel to keep the control over her life that she had hitherto exercised. After leaving school, Caroline had spent a year abroad perfecting her French, punctuating this period with visits home to coincide with school holidays. Meriel found it pleasant to have an attractive grown-up daughter, particularly one who proved so easily malleable; and Caroline, fair and slight, resembled her mother so little that neither detracted in the least from the other. The daughter, pretty and gay, had blossomed as a credit to her upbringing. After a secretarial course in London she had worked for a firm of estate agents, and she had left there to become secretary to a television director; she was now his assistant. Meriel had not approved of this change : she thought the estate agency suitably respectable, but television smacked, to her, of the bizarre, and she frowned to think of the people with whom Caroline would mix.

Caroline laughed at her mother's views, called her a die-hard, and said that selling houses bored her. She had secured her new job through the aid of a friend, and found that it was never dull; interesting people surrounded her, and she was happy. Till this change she had returned home nearly every weekend, but now her hours varied and she sometimes worked on Sundays. She still came home quite often for her time off in the week, but Meriel could not grow used to this lack of order and regularity. She found it hard to show enthusiasm when her own friends seemed to think Caroline fortunate in finding this niche.

Various young men figured briefly in Caroline's life, but she seemed to take none of them very seriously. Meriel hoped that she would marry Gerald Manners, the son of Felicity who was to come to lunch today. He was a rising young industrialist who already owned a Sunbeam Rapier and would clearly in time rise to a Bentley. On all possible occasions the two young people were thrown together, but so far Caroline, who had known Gerald for most of her life, seemed easily able to resist his charms. They met in London sometimes; but

29

Caroline had no lack of invitations either at home or in town. Hanni, admiringly, would declare : 'Caroline is too gay, she won't marry for years. Much better she should enjoy herself and be free.' Meriel did not approve these sentiments; when she was a girl, early marriage was a sign of success, and she did not want the reflection of failure; nor did she understand the lure of independence. The commotion of a large wedding was a pleasure to which she looked forward; she saw herself making a success in the role of bride's mother, and she faced with equanimity the prospect of being a grandmother for this would increase her range of influence into another generation.

Among her letters this birthday morning, accompanying a rather sentimental card, was one from Phoebe Jenkins with whom Meriel had been at school. Their paths had seldom crossed since those days, but Phoebe, now widowed and a grandmother, would not relinquish the strands of a friendship which to Meriel had worn itself down into mere nuisance value. Appropriate cards arrived faithfully on all occasions, usually enclosing long, rambling letters about Phoebe's own family and comparing them unfavourably with Meriel's apparently more successful children. Phoebe bewailed poor scholastic progress, and adopted a trying humility about later achievements. Meriel enjoyed the feeling of superiority which Phoebe never failed to provoke in her, but otherwise she found the prolonged relationship a weary bore and wished Phoebe too

would tire of it. Today, however, her constancy made
some amends for Caroline's defection.

'—and now another birthday comes along,' Phoebe
wrote. 'Goodness, it seems no time at all since your
twenty-first. Do you remember that wonderful dance
your parents gave for you? You wore yellow, and I
had my pink, new, it was, for the occasion, and a piece
of wild extravagance. I'd been married two years, and
felt very grown-up and grand, but it was obvious you
wouldn't be long. Peter was never far from your side
all evening. Now here am I, all alone, no Roger, Betty
married and in Scotland and Jack in Canada. But
you've got everything. I hope you'll always have it. I
always said you were born to be lucky, and now
you've got that lovely house, dear Peter coming home
to you every evening, sweet Caroline her mother's girl,
and dear little Rupert almost a baby still, such a pet.
They'll never go far away, that I know, and soon
you'll have grandchildren too. They're such a joy. I
had baby Veronica to stay a week ago, and she's coming again in the summer when Betty and Hugh go to
Italy—' Impatiently, Meriel crumpled the letter,
written in a large, flowing hand, and threw it down.
She did not want to read Phoebe's vapid maunderings
about her grandchild's latest tooth, and she did not
care whether Betty and Hugh went to Timbuctoo. It
was life in Timpsley that mattered to her, and the life
of herself most of all.

She got up from the table and took her cards into

the drawing-room where she arranged them in a row on the white-painted mantelpiece. Then she stood back to admire the effect. It was pleasant to see so many manifestations of affection; she spared even a moment of gratitude for Phoebe. She could afford to be generous. She was still basking in a glow of self-congratulation when Rupert came into the room, reading a book. Sensing that she was there, he looked up from it as he kicked the door to behind him; hastily he snapped it shut. Meriel forbore to comment, but she folded her lips together in what Rupert had begun to describe to himself as 'her *moue*', an expression he had lately discovered.

'Hi, Mum,' he greeted her.

Meriel relented. 'Hi yourself,' she said. 'Where are you off to?'

'Well, I was going to have a bit of a read,' said Rupert, defensively.

'What about Martian?' asked his mother. She crossed to the window and looked out at the rain. 'It's slackening,' she declared optimistically. 'Take him out first, Rupert. It's more important. You can read later.'

'Let's compromise,' suggested Rupert bravely. He was remembering his mission in the village. It could not be carried out until the shops opened. 'I'll just read to the end of this act that I'm in, and then I'll go out. O.K.?'

'Oh, very well.' Meriel gave in. Still *Hamlet*, she

supposed. 'But mind you do. Don't get carried away so that you forget to stop.'

'I won't,' Rupert promised. He drew his forefinger across his throat in a garrotting gesture, and flung himself down on to the sofa with his feet up and his head down. Immediately he was at Elsinore.

Meriel went upstairs to have her bath. Her morning ritual seldom varied, and she was rarely ready for the day before ten o'clock. If she went up to London, the upheaval necessary to achieve her early start threw the whole house into a turmoil. The boiler, thanks to the ministrations of Peter and Hanni, was now ready to supply many gallons of hot water; Meriel cast a liberal handful of her despised new bath salts into it, and was soon immersed, with only her head, crowned with a green spotted plastic cap, above the tide.

A hearty thump at the door startled her out of a pleasant doze. It was Rupert.

'I'm going out now,' he announced. 'Goodbye.'

'Goodbye,' she called back drowsily, and began lazily to soap an arm. Perhaps Rupert was right, and one of those long-handled bath brushes would be a nice thing to have.

Below, in the kitchen, Hanni was clattering about, still singing. She had finished washing up the breakfast things by the time Mrs. Fawcett, who came daily to clean, arrived.

' 'Morning,' said Mrs. Fawcett, creaking in through

the back door in her mackintosh and wellingtons. 'What a day. Should have brought me punt, I reckon.'

'Terrible, isn't it,' Hanni agreed brightly. 'Never mind, it'll pass.'

' "Rain before seven, fine by eleven", they say,' said Mrs. Fawcett. 'Still, they're not always right. Can't think how you can stand it, coming from where you do.' This was, indeed, one of Mrs. Fawcett's constant causes for wonder.

'I don't mind,' said Hanni. 'It's warm in the house, and soon it will be summer.' She began to get bowls from the cupboard and set them on the table for lunch preparations.

'Well, talking won't mend it, and I'd best get along,' said Mrs. Fawcett, who by this time had removed her wet outer garments and was revealed in a flowered overall. 'Brass today, chronic it gets in the damp. See you later.'

'Surely,' said Hanni, who had polished up her English at the cinema.

Mrs. Fawcett, leaving the kitchen with her hands full of cleaning materials, collided violently with Rupert on his way out of the house by his usual route.

'Hullo, Mrs. Fawcett, how're you? Sorry,' he said, disentangling himself from the Hoover and mop which she was carrying well to the fore like a shield, and knocking the tin of Brasso out of her grasp.

'Someone's in a hurry,' said Mrs. Fawcett mildly,

34

graciously accepting the tin which Rupert retrieved. 'Where are you off to?'

'I'm just buzzing off into Timpsley on my bike for Dad. Then I'm going for a ride,' said Rupert.

'What, going out on your pony in all this rain?' cried Mrs. Fawcett. 'The poor thing.'

'Martian's out in it anyway in his field,' Rupert pointed out. 'He never shelters in his shed except when it's hot. He needs exercise, it'll warm him up.'

'And so do you, I suppose,' said Mrs. Fawcett. 'Well, it takes all kinds, doesn't it?' She shuffled off into the hall with her heavy load. Rupert lounged across the kitchen.

'Anything you want, Hanni?' he asked. He was wearing an old oilskin, relic of a sailing holiday.

'No, Rupert, thank you. Your mother went to the shops yesterday and we have all ordered for lunch. No dinner to prepare tonight as they're going out to celebrate—will you go, this time, do you think? Or will it be eggs and bacon with Hanni like always?'

'Oh, I shan't go—it's a parents-only tradition, children to be left in the nursery,' said Rupert. 'But thank goodness it is, I'd hate to go. Sure to be terribly smoky there, it always is in places where you eat.'

Hanni thought this a sweeping pronouncement, but she let it pass. She knew how the smell of tobacco smoke irritated Rupert and had often seen him glaring at his mother's ceaseless stream of cigarettes.

'Well, off you go now, I'm busy,' she said.

'What's for lunch?' Rupert dawdled by the door.

'Chicken, with new potatoes and young carrots, and coffee soufflé,' said Hanni. 'Mrs. Manners is coming.'

'Oh, heck! Can I have mine out here?' Rupert asked, standing on one leg.

'Well, it's your mother's birthday, I should think she'll want you with her,' said Hanni, who would have if she had been in Meriel's place. 'But you could ask her.'

Rupert made a face. 'I'm sure she won't, they'd much rather natter without me to hear their scandal and gossip,' he said. 'Couldn't you say, "You won't be wanting Rupert, I'll give him his lunch in the kitchen"?' he begged. 'It'll be deadly. They won't talk to me. They'll be on about that play they're going to act.'

'Well, you'll enjoy that,' said Hanni. 'You like plays.'

'Yes, I do, but they don't,' said Rupert. 'It doesn't mean anything to them, it's just an excuse.'

'Excuse?' This was too involved for Hanni's simple philosophy.

'An excuse for going out to lunch with each other, and having tea parties, and making a lot of fuss.' He glowered. 'Please, Hanni. Have a bash.'

'All right, I'll try, but don't count on it,' said Hanni.

'Thanks.' He grinned at her. 'You're wonderful, Hanni. I don't know what I'd do without you.' He went away, leaving the door wide open behind him. Hanni watched him slop through the puddles in the yard to the garage, where his bicycle was kept. His hair was already wet and plastered to his head, and the rain ran in rivulets off his oilskin. She called after him.

'Hey, Rupert, put something on your head.'

He looked round, already far away in his imagination, and put a hand up to his head.

'Waste of time, it's wet already,' he said, and continued on his way. Hanni stood, hands on hips, looking after him despairingly with a rueful expression; she waited until he rode past, head well down, on his smart blue bicycle. Then she closed the door, turned back to the table and began stuffing the chicken. While she worked, she wondered how many days it would be before a letter came for her from Franz, a medical student she had met on her last visit home.

Rupert, free-wheeling down the hill into Timpsley, was composing in his head:

> 'There was an old girl, Mrs. Fawcett,
> Who needed a wash and of course it
> Was eau from the tap
> That she used, she's a chap
> Uninformed about faucets, is Fawcett.'

He was well pleased with this, despite the inevitability of referring to a woman as a chap; he was not the first poet to resort to desperate measures in the interests of form.

Mrs. Fawcett herself, now in the drawing-room, was

having a good look at all Meriel's cards. She picked
each one up carefully and read the printed sentiments
diligently, as well as the signatures of the senders. In
most cases she knew exactly who they all were, and
frowned or smiled at the aptness of the greetings, nod-
ding her head at some of the verses.

'Wonder what he gave her?' she mused, plugging in
the Hoover. 'Something grand, that I know. Lucky
woman, there's some as don't know when they're well
off.' She heard Hanni's voice, upraised in melody
again, and smiled. 'Someone's happy, anyhow,' she
said aloud, and switched on.

Meriel made the beds, hers and Peter's. This was
the only domestic task she performed, except in the
rare spells when either Hanni or Mrs. Fawcett ailed.
Rupert was supposed to make his own, but usually he
simply pulled the sheets back into a semblance of order
and covered the result with his yellow candlewick bedspread. Sometimes Meriel inspected it and made him
return to do it properly after first stripping it herself.
Sometimes Hanni or Mrs. Fawcett, dusting his room,
secretly remade it. After she came downstairs for the
second time each day, Meriel went into the kitchen to
discuss the meals with Hanni, and then she telephoned
the local shops which delivered for anything that must
be ordered. Twice a week she drove into Timpsley for
what could not be obtained by remote command in
this way. The rest of her day was free for the develop-

ment of her own life; and to fill in the idle hours, she had evolved, like the other women of her age who were no longer limited by the demands of small children who must be fetched from and delivered to day-schools, a formula which left little real leisure, kept her on the go, and was in itself to some, satisfying. The younger women were busy: their more dependent children filled their days; but Meriel and her contemporaries existed simply for bridge, coffee parties and the Women's Institute, which had in Timpsley become largely a club for the well-to-do middle class rather than the representative gathering it was designed to be, and the Drama Group.

Today, Meriel was going out to coffee at Edith Browne's. Edith was a pillar of local society, the wife of a retired General, and the centre or focal point of most functions. To be 'in' with her was to have arrived, and Meriel had been in this happy position for many years. She was a frequent visitor at The Grange, a mausoleum built on a knoll above Timpsley Common. This morning's was merely a social gathering with no hidden purpose, but sometimes Edith invited people because she proposed to dragoon them into serving her by helping with the British Legion fête or arranging whist drives in aid of the Red Cross. Timpsley expended a certain amount of its energy in these laudable directions.

Before getting the car out, Meriel, an umbrella up over her head, went down to the paddock at the end of the garden. It was owned by a local farmer who for a small sum undertook responsibility for Martian in term-time when Rupert was away. The pony, a grey, with a small, mean head, glared at her from a distance and made no move to approach. Meriel frowned. Where was Rupert? He should have been here, catching the animal. In fact, she had intended to help him, for Martian did not surrender his person easily and took some time to capture. She turned away, annoyed. He was probably spinning out time by day-dreaming in the garden shed where he kept the halter and the rest of the tack. She did not go and look, but went on to the garage and got out her car.

This morning, it was her duty to collect Winifred Gray, who was also invited out to coffee at The Grange and had no car of her own. Each morning her husband took the family Ford to the station, and Winifred was left marooned apart from the infrequent buses and her bicycle. She was not ready when Meriel arrived, and thrust her chauffeuse into a chair with the paper while she despatched a few final chores. Unlike Meriel, she had only sketchy help in the house; she was a first-class cook and spent happy hours growing herbs, fruit and vegetables in order that she might spend more happy hours preparing them for the table. Today she had begun some baking before Meriel arrived, and her schedule had run late since she had yielded to the temptation to make just one batch of angel cakes.

Resigned, Meriel accepted *The Daily Telegraph* and sat down by the fire until she should be ready. Winifred had never yet been punctual in all the years they had known each other.

When at last they drove along the narrow, wet road dividing the common, below Timpsley Grange, they passed a solitary figure trotting along on a pony. Rupert had somehow caught Martian, saddled him, and was out for his ride.

3

At eight o'clock on the morning of Meriel's birthday, Joan Bentham was summoned from the task of making her bed by the shrill scream of the kettle, whistling that it was boiling. She pulled her green folk-weave bedspread into position and hurried into the small kitchen of her flat, which was on the top floor of a gaunt house in an unfashionable district of London where rents still remained in reasonable proportion to salaries. Clouds of steam issued from the kettle as it continued to pierce the damp morning air with its tocsin. Joan put a heaped spoonful of Instant Coffee into a breakfast cup and poured on the boiling water; the mixture frothed slightly as she stirred, and then subsided; she added milk and sugar, and took a gulping mouthful before lighting the grill to make toast. Then she hurried back into the bedroom, picked her dressing-gown up from a chair and hung it on the back of the door, and still in her stockinged feet, carried her shoes out into the kitchen. She rubbed them up while the second side of her toast browned, and when it was ready she put it on a tray already laid, topped up her coffee with more hot water, and carried her repast into the sitting-room. Her kitchen was so small that there was not enough room in it for a chair.

Joan set the tray down on a low table, spread butter and marmalade on her toast and took a bite; then she crossed to the window and gazed outside at the depressing prospect. It was raining hard, and the pavement gleamed with the wet. It was too early for many people to be about in the quiet road, but one or two cars passed, and a few umbrellas could be seen hurrying along below, the feet of their owners appearing briefly under them as they walked. She turned away and switched on the wireless; then she sat down on the small sofa and went on with her breakfast.

After a few seconds an unctuous female voice was heard:

'Fish is plentiful, though inclined to be dear,' it declared. 'Landings of cod are large: look for the smaller bream and haddock, they are good value and can be economical for those on a limited budget—' Muttering, Joan got up, licking a marmalade-y finger, and switched off the wireless. She pictured the speaker as spectacled and plain, with a complacent dowdiness and clutching a holdall. This she knew was unfair; if the truth were known, the shopping expert doubtless combined glamour and chic with her market wisdom, but Joan could not be enthusiastic about cod or cauliflower at this hour, and the evasively phrased pointers to thrift irritated her; she thought she would enjoy

43

hearing advice to millionaires on how best to buy caviare and yachts. How many people listened to or heeded the wise words she had rejected, Joan wondered. She could not imagine a million housewives tuned in attentively. Then she decided that perhaps her view was simply prejudiced because there was no one in her life for whom she must seek out culinary bargains. She seldom entertained; if she did have anyone to dinner she offered them expensive, because trouble-free, menus, prepared chiefly from frozen ingredients in the short time she had available after work. She had a good lunch herself every day, with luncheon vouchers provided as a 'perk' to her job; most evenings her supper was of a somewhat sketchy variety, for it seemed wasted effort to take trouble for herself. She sighed as she thought about this, and drank her coffee; then she hurried back into the cupboard-like kitchen, where she quickly rinsed plate, cup, saucer, spoon and knife, and left them to drain on a plastic rack. Then she went back to her bedroom to do her face and her hair.

Joan was a very ordinary woman of thirty-five. She had hair of an indeterminate shade of brown, brown eyes, and a pale complexion with fine-textured skin that now showed increasing lines. She had a straight nose of medium length, and a wide, rather generous mouth which did not look as though it had been intended to be folded firmly shut in the disciplined manner that was being more and more practised by its owner. She was not tall, nor short either; and though not really thin, neither was she plump. She would never be noticed in a group; all her life she had been overlooked because there were always so many people more striking than she was. She had learned to be content with her negative attributes; she never expected much from life, and so she was seldom disappointed. She had two or three girl-friends of whom she was fond, and for whom she would take trouble; she had elderly parents now retired to a cottage in Berkshire where she occasionally spent weekends; and she had a brother who was a successful engineer and whom she seldom saw, which was a pity as she had a great affection for his children, her small nieces and her nephew. She had held various jobs before her present one, working for a doctor and then a professor of ancient history, but she had been in her present post for ten years now. She knew herself to be efficient, and she was paid a salary which also recognised this. She had never received a proposal of marriage in her life, though proposals of other kinds were not unknown to her. She had been for years deeply in love with her employer.

At twenty-five minutes to nine exactly, Joan left her flat. She wore a proofed tweed coat and carried an umbrella; a scarf was tied over her head, and she had plastic boots on over her shoes, but even so her stockings were splashed at the back as she hurried to the bus stop at the end of the road.

On the bus, she glanced quickly at the headlines of *The Daily Telegraph*, which had been thrust into her letter-box earlier. She would read it properly this evening; most days she read it at lunch, but she would not be alone today, as it was Wednesday. Soon she put the paper away in her capacious bag, and composed her thoughts towards the hours ahead. There were one or two problems still remaining from the previous day to be sorted out, and the morning's letters would be sure to contain more. But also she had made a resolution which must be carried out without relenting, whatever opposition it met. She was going to give notice.

Joan was only twenty-five when she first met the man for whom she worked now. She had been a temporary replacement in the office, during holiday absences, while she filled in time herself between the history professor and finding a new permanent job. At the end of her month someone had left to get married, and she had been asked to stay on; she had agreed, at first intending to leave after a year, but soon she had become absorbed into the place until she lost the energy and the desire to go; after that she began to enjoy the prestige that came of having her ability appreciated. She did not know herself when it was that she had fallen in love; she simply realised one day that she was no longer hoping to meet her fate in the bus queue, at a cocktail party or at the theatre, as hitherto. Vaguely, she supposed that she was becoming a careerist and giving her job the importance she had once attached to dreams of romance and a family; she hid behind this illusion for a long time, until she was forced to diagnose her condition.

On the surface everything had been quite normal. The day had been a long one, and she had been late finishing the letters. When she took them into the office for signing he was over by the window, staring out. He did not turn immediately as she came in, and so she had made a small noise as she crossed the room, to attract his attention inconspicuously. He had swung round then and smiled, rubbing his hand across his forehead and eyes in a way that betrayed his fatigue, yet made him look curiously defenceless and rather like the small son whose photograph stood on his desk.

'Ah, Joan,' was all he had said at first. He had not looked at his letters, but merely signed them quickly, one after the other. 'You never err,' he'd added, and she had smiled too, waiting beside him as she had done hundreds of times before until he reached the end of the pile. Then he looked up at her, tilting his chair back. 'I've kept you late again. I'm sorry, Joan.'

'That's quite all right,' she had protested. "It doesn't matter.'

'You won't be late for whatever you're doing this evening?'

'I'm not going anywhere,' she had replied, gathering up the letters. Then she had suddenly noticed how tired he looked, and that his hair needed cutting. An extraordinary sensation had gone through her, and she had felt a violent urge to put down the papers and clasp him against her Marks and Spencer's blouse. The mad impulse had passed as swiftly as it had come as she sternly went on with piling up the mail, but after that evening she began to be aware of how she waited each morning for his arrival, fifteen minutes after her own, and the sound of his step in the passage. His head would appear round her office door and he would say: ''Morning, Joan. I'm here. When you're ready.' She could not remember when he had begun this habit: it had not always happened; at first he had simply rung for her to go along with the letters when he was in his own office. Now, after his announcement, she waited long enough to let him travel the length of the passage and install himself behind his desk; then she followed and they would begin the day's work.

After her moment of revelation nothing had changed; she pretended to herself that it had not happened. He was married, happily as far as she knew, and she certainly hoped it was so; this was something that just did not happen. Good secretaries might be devoted to their bosses in the line of duty, but not outside that. Besides, she wasn't the type. But time passed, and with it her acceptance grew. Her whole life centred round the eight or nine hours that she spent every day in his service.

For years he had called her by her Christian name,

but naturally she had never used his. Then one evening, when once again they were late and he had missed his usual train, suddenly he had burst out: 'God, I'm tired.'

Joan had never heard him complain aloud before on his own account, though he grumbled about other things. She saw now as she turned to look at him that he did indeed seem utterly weary.

'Poor Peter, you are, aren't you?' she had said in concern.

Surprisingly, his face had lightened, and he laughed. 'Well, you've done it at last,' he exclaimed. 'You've called me Peter.' And then he kissed her. At first she was too stunned to feel even amazement, but after a few moments she was in no state to analyse her thoughts. They had released each other eventually, and turned away from one another, Joan with her hand to her lips. Peter was the first to speak.

'I—er, we'd better forget that, I think,' he said.

'Yes, of course,' Joan had mumbled.

'I don't quite know what happened,' Peter went on, in fact very far from forgetting.

'It doesn't matter. It's not important,' Joan said.

But it was important. Neither could forget it, though on the surface all was as before. Joan, though ashamed of herself, longed for the moment to be repeated; while unknown to her, Peter contrasted her warm, generous lips with Meriel's tight, narrow little mouth that seemed to grow daily more close. For a while Joan

juggled with the idea of leaving : conscience advised
it, but she knew she would be hard to replace; she was
more of an assistant than a secretary now. As the
weeks went uneventfully by she relaxed. Alone, she
endured torment; but she got satisfaction from her
efforts to ensure that everything possible was done to
make the office run smoothly. She grew learned in the
law, and Peter told her she ought to become articled.

But now, like a question mark in her mind, was the
image of Meriel. They had met, of course, though
rarely. Joan had thought her pleasant and attractive,
though she had rather resented her condescension.
Meriel spoke to her in a very *grande dame* manner.
Peter never mentioned her, though he spoke often of
Rupert and Caroline, both of whose careers Joan followed keenly. She began to fear that Peter's marriage
was less successful than she had supposed.

A year went by. Both had lapsed back into their
normal behaviour, except that when they were alone
Joan now allowed herself the luxury, very occasionally, of using his Christian name. Without realising
what she did, she let her voice linger over the two
syllables, like a caress. And then of course, inevitably,
it happened again. Joan had a bad headache; in fact,
she was at the beginning of an attack of 'flu. Peter,
noticing her pallor and the obvious fact that she was
ill, challenged her. Weakly, she admitted that she felt
wretched, and there she was once again in his arms,
but this time weeping feebly. She stopped quite

quickly, and he mopped her up and sent her back to her flat in a taxi, in the charge of one of the other girls from the office. But in the evening he called to see her himself, bearing a large bunch of grapes as an excuse.

So they were undone. At first he pretended both to himself and to her that he was calling in only to see how she was, because she lived alone; and she pretended that the deception did not matter because at the beginning she felt too ill to cope with something so difficult. When she was better she found that they had jumped several hurdles of reserve and entered upon a degree of communion that was too precious for either to break. Before long a routine developed: they lunched together regularly once a week on Wednesdays, unless any professional commitment of Peter's prevented it. Once, when Meriel was away staying with one of her brothers, they spent an idyllic weekend together in the New Forest. Occasionally, Peter pretended to Meriel that he had a duty dinner engagement, and he spent the evening in the flat at the top of the tall house.

Several times Joan, made wretched by her conscience, attempted to end the affair, but each time she let herself be persuaded to go on, because that was what she really wanted, herself. She wasted no sympathy on Meriel; now that she understood how cavalierly Peter was treated at home she felt no pity for his wife, but she knew that he himself was ridden with guilt. He would never leave Meriel: for a short time Joan had fed herself daydreams in which he did, so that in due time they could marry; but in the clear dawn of reality she knew he would never willingly chip or crack Meriel's glass case, where she lived exposed to the world as a perfect wife and mother with every material benefit. He thought that Meriel could not exist without the elaborations of her life.

Now, Joan had decided to end the whole thing. She admitted to herself that the love Peter felt for her was little more than gratitude. She had happened to be near, familiar and safe, at a time when his unhappy loneliness was deepest; that was all. He would never have gone out deliberately to seek for someone sympathetic; she, by being so vulnerable herself, had been largely to blame. Through him she had experienced great joy, but it could not go on. Better to end it now, before Peter wanted to and could not find a way. All that was required was some strength of mind. She had resolved to leave the office at the end of a month's notice; one of the other girls could easily be promoted into her place, and in time would know as much as Joan did now. At the end of that month Joan would go abroad for a long holiday, perhaps to Switzerland or Italy. When she had first worked for Peter she had been in the way of going abroad for a fortnight every year, and spending her third week's holiday with her parents, but latterly this custom had lapsed and she had spent most of her time down in Berkshire, fretting to get back.

The bus reached her stop and Joan got out. She walked quickly down the street towards the office. 'Let me stick to it,' she prayed silently. 'Let me be firm.'

She would go away for at least a month, and then she would get a new job, far away, perhaps in America. Anyway, not in London, where she would expect to meet Peter at every turn.

She entered the doorway of the building where Peter's firm had their offices on the second floor, and went into the lift. Five minutes later she was seated in front of her typewriter finishing a long and complicated report of some recent litigation.

4

PETER travelled up to London each day in company with a number of men whom he knew either personally or by sight, because they were neighbours or because they had all used the same train service for years. Today, Meriel's birthday, was no different; the commuters nodded and greeted each other with friendliness, but beyond a few muttered comments on the weather there was little conversation; they all unfurled newspapers or opened briefcases, lighted pipes or cigarettes, and settled down to occupy the journey profitably. Peter, however, remembering Rupert's attempt at avoiding his ride, began to wonder about the reason. The boy was lucky to own a pony, though to be sure Martian was a wilful little brute at times. Peter himself knew nothing about horses except what he had gleaned during the years in which his children had ridden; but Meriel's family had always been used to owning them, and she was the moving spirit behind the equine activities at Merelands. Caroline had certainly been content, as a schoolgirl, to spend most of her time either on her pony's back or grooming it, or cleaning its tack. Rupert had followed along behind her, and last summer had won several rosettes at local gymkhanas, for Martian, when in the mood, was a good jumper, and could sometimes be persuaded to excel at bending or in the other competitions organised on these occasions. Peter had always assumed that he enjoyed all this; now he began to wonder. He knew that the pony had become difficult to catch lately, and he had been nipped several times himself when he had been harmlessly attempting to pat Martian in a friendly way. Long months of idleness, eating his head off in the field on a diet well supplemented by the farmer whom Meriel paid to undertake the care of the animal, obviously did him no good. It occurred to Peter that he knew very little of what went on in his son's mind, and that perhaps he was not alone in trying to conform to the pattern expected of him. Certainly it was true that he and Rupert had lately shared several moments of communication, such as the two occasions this morning when they had been united over the need to make Meriel's birthday a success.

Rupert had always been an easy, amenable child, not given to spectacular achievement in any direction, but progressing at an adequate speed along the prescribed scholastic path before him. He was not particularly good at games, but he seemed to enjoy playing them and was by no means a failure where sports were concerned. Peter had always thought of him as an average boy, and hoped that one day he would join him in the firm; however, if his bent lay in another

direction, then all possible would be done by his father
to allow it to be followed. He knew that Meriel did
not remotely understand Rupert's present preoccupation with poetry and drama; she thought it unfortun-
ate and was sure it would lead to moods and brooding.
Rupert, in her view, ought to be a rugger or cricket
maniac; and since he was neither she assumed he was
horse mad and encouraged him to develop the obses-
sion. Boys needed occupying, and riding was certainly
a healthy way to spend time that otherwise might hang
heavy; but Peter himself in his youth, when there was
time for it, had loved music and spent hours at sym-
phony concerts : after a few attempts he had given up
trying to persuade Meriel to share his interest, and
had abandoned it himself; he had some sympathy for
Rupert's tastes.

It seemed, now, that riding might not be after all
the abiding love it had appeared; Peter resolved to
talk to the boy about it, and made a note in his diary :
'R. and M. ?Golf,' for here was another way Rupert
might be better employed than careering about on a
pony he possibly disliked. It was certainly not worth
keeping Martian, at considerable expense, if it was a
penance to Rupert to ride, though it would not be easy
to get Meriel to share this opinion. Peter wondered
why, if Rupert did not enjoy his riding, he did not tell
his mother; and his heart sank at the thought that he
and the boy shared a conspiracy to maintain Meriel's
complacent happiness at all costs.

Sitting in the train, Peter shuffled his feet at these uncomfortable ideas. Hugh Wheeler, sitting opposite him, looked up from the sheets of figures resting on his knee and grinned. Peter grinned back and sighed; here was another manifestation of his own weakness and deceitfulness. Meriel did not approve of Hugh and his wife : both had been married before, both had passed through the divorce court; each had children of their previous marriages who came and went at frequent intervals on visits to the rather untidy little house at the other side of Timpsley village. Peter, after several years, had grown friendly with Hugh as a result of travelling with him each day; he liked the other man's wideawake, receptive mind, his vision and his tolerance. Now they sometimes met in town for lunch; and sometimes, on the way home from the station, Peter dropped in at the Wheelers' house for a drink. He never stayed long; he never told Meriel. He never made any excuses to Hugh and Stella for not inviting them to Merelands : the situation, never discussed, was fully understood by all three. Meriel's attitude was not held as a result of Hugh and Stella's earlier marital misfortunes, though she sometimes said that because of these they were doubtless 'not sound'. They met at parties in the district, for the Wheelers had a lot of friends; they were gay and sociable, and clearly so happy in each other's company that less fortunate couples envied them and hoped by contact that they might catch the infection and discover how to share their joy. Meriel's objection was never specified aloud : it was simply that the Wheelers were not wealthy, and neither were they nobly born, so that to know them would not advance the Grahams in any way; and though it was possible to condescend towards them, they seemed unaware that they should be grateful for notice. They were completely incapable of appreciating the subtleties of the local social strata, and therefore they were invulnerable to the Timpsley élite.

Sometimes, if Meriel was out or away and he did not stay in London, Peter spent occasional evenings with Hugh and Stella. There was harmony in their house; Stella was a good cook and a warm-hearted hostess. Peter met pleasant people there whom he never met anywhere else, couples still unspoiled by the rat race. He supposed it was possible to retain one's integrity in the teeth of success; but he recognised that the mutual effort of striving to attain a position sometimes united those who otherwise had little other common ground. When the urge was removed, the bonds slackened. He did not often think like this, for he was not greatly given to introspection; in fact it was Stella, speaking in analogies, who had first made him follow this line of thought.

Because both had been through much unhappiness before they came together, Hugh and Stella greatly prized their present contentment, and were determined never to take it for granted. Now, Stella was pregnant, and this was a new reason for joy. Meriel, meeting her in the street and observing her condition for herself, thought it 'most unnecessary', but Peter knew how much they both wanted a child that was theirs, though they loved the other children who spent much of their time in their house.

Peter knew that Stella was often tired and overworked, and that money was tight, but she was always welcoming and responsive; he sighed, thinking of Joan, who was the same. Hugh glanced up at him again above his work: poor old Peter, life was a bit hard for him and he looked as though already he had had enough of the day.

In the tube, where they continued together with their journey, Peter confessed to Hugh that he had forgotten to buy Meriel a birthday present. He was greatly tempted to indulge himself further and confess also to the disgraceful fact that he was sordidly having an affair with his secretary, for he longed for the relief of unburdening himself, and if there was anyone who would hear him in sympathy and respect his confidence, Hugh was that person. But he did not.

Hugh, however, was properly aghast at the enormity of Peter's sin of omission.

'What on earth can I get her?' he appealed.

Hugh thought of all the things he would like to give Stella. They varied from a diamond and ruby ring to a car, some expensive scent, orchids, and a négligée. Aloud, he suggested the négligée and knew it was a mistake even as the word left his lips, for Peter's expression tightened at once.

'I told her it wasn't ready and that I was collecting it today,' he said. 'It'll have to be something that could have been got specially.' He did not elaborate on the unsuitability of Hugh's idea.

'A bag, with her initials on it?' Hugh tried, ever anxious to help.

Peter brightened. That was a possibility. Finnegan's or some such place would probably be able to accomplish something like that in a matter of hours.

'Or how about a poodle?' went on Hugh, now carried away by the limitless possibilities. He and Stella had discussed Meriel and pitied Peter for the emptiness of his home life. Together, they laughed at Meriel, who typified in their opinion all that was worst in feminine middle-class materialism. They had often wondered why she did not have a tiresome little dog tittupping at her heels to make her character complete. Stella would giggle and say that she had Peter to run after her, but Hugh would then declare that Peter got none of the cossetting a poodle would require.

'I say, I believe you've got it!' Peter was seriously taking up the proposal that had been made half in mockery. Hugh felt abashed.

'I believe you've got something there,' Peter went on. At least such a gift would be evidence of trouble taken; he could say to Meriel that he had got it to keep her company, for she was often alone at home, apart from Hanni. The Swiss girl would look after it if Meriel was out. Joan would know where to get one, or she would soon find out : he never, as a matter of principle, asked her to get anything that Meriel required unless it was unavoidable, but this time he would have to enlist her aid in discovering a poodle breeder or purveyor from whom he could get a dog today. He felt greatly relieved at having reached a solution to his problems, and beamed his farewell at Hugh when they parted.

Now, getting near his office and with this decision taken, Peter's mind returned to affairs of business. He knew, as he walked the last few hundred yards, that Joan would be completing a report for him for a complicated case they were handling. Once again he blessed his good fortune in having her assistance. If she were ever to leave him, he knew she would be able to obtain an executive position commanding a much higher salary than she received now. By thinking of her professional talents he tried to prevent his mind from returning to the other aspect of their relationship. Whenever he let himself dwell on this he became bogged in a morass of muddled thought and vain regrets. Really, it would have been much more comfortable if the whole thing had never got beyond that first moment of revelation in the office; but the trouble was, once you admitted the possibility of something like this happening, it became easy to slide a little

61

further, and then a little further, until nothing was impossible and a reason could be found to justify everything.

Peter did not consider that Meriel was being harmed in any way by his association with Joan. What they shared was something that had no value for Meriel. To her, he was merely the provider, the rung by which she climbed, the necessary acquisition if children were to be produced. She would never know he was unfaithful to her because it would never occur to her that he could be; but if she were to discover, it would be her pride, and not her heart that would be hurt.

No, the harm came from what this was doing to Joan, and perhaps even to himself, through the degradation of maintaining a deception. He owed her so much, for through her he had developed a sort of confidence, and an ability to detach himself from his home background. But it never seriously crossed his mind that he might leave Meriel and, in the fullness of time, marry Joan, thereby winning for himself a home like Hugh's. Other people did that sort of thing, but not Peter. Meriel could never be placed in that position.

Peter worried, often, about Joan's future. It was something they never discussed; when they were together they lived only for the present. But he could give her no security or open recognition; all that he could do was to provide some extra comfort for her flat if he noticed it was lacking. He knew, with humility, that she loved him to the exclusion of every-one else in her life; and because he could not make her of the same importance to him, he felt always as if he must seek other ways to make it up to her. Though he sometimes wished, for the sake of his peace of mind, that the affair had never begun, at other times he knew it was his life-line. It helped him to put up a façade at home, for home no longer really mattered to him, or had the power to hurt. He blamed himself for losing Meriel's love, not realising that in fact he had never really had it, for real love was not in her to give.

He hurried into the office building, up the stairs, through the hall and into the lift. Soon he was push-ing open the swing door with the name, Graham and Linnit, written on it in yellowing paint, and a moment later he had opened the door of Joan's office and poked his head round it. She looked up at once from her typewriter, for she had been listening for his foot-steps, and she smiled. Her face was paler than usual; she was tired, he thought, with a rare contraction of the heart. He knew her drab little breakfast routine, and was suddenly conscious of all the solitary morn-ings and evenings she had spent already and of how many more lay ahead, for while she loved him there was no rescue for her. He at least was seldom alone, though he often thought solitude would be preferable to dancing in Meriel's wake. Sometimes he thought he could be utterly happy alone upon an island, where there were no claims on him and no more obligations.

Instead of withdrawing his head and going at once along the corridor to his own office after indicating that he had arrived, Peter, on impulse, walked inside Joan's, closed the door firmly behind him and strode purposefully over to her. Then he proceeded to kiss her very determinedly, for the moment not even caring if one of the typists or the junior partner were to walk in.

5

CAROLINE GRAHAM shared with two other girls a flat that had been converted from part of a large house in a Kensington square. By pooling their resources they were able to afford a degree of comfort impossible for one alone; they also pooled many of their clothes, so that each was able to appear in a wide range of outfits and something could be found that was apt for any occasion. If one was ill, the others looked after her with devotion, although normally storms, tantrums and tensions often seethed among the trio; any hint of adversity to one caused the ranks to close, however, and all were united wholly until the crisis had passed.

On her mother's birthday Caroline was up early. Her bed was piled with dresses, stockings and underclothes in disarray, and two suitcases stood open on the floor. Tissue paper floated round her feet as she hurried to and fro taking more things from her cupboards and drawers and adding them to the general confusion. Now and then she paused in indecision to gaze at the chaos she had made, hand to head, her fair hair framing a soft, still childish face.

Along the passage, Daphne, whose turn it was to prepare breakfast, clattered about in the kitchen brewing coffee and boiling eggs. The sound of scraping came as she scratched the charred crumbs off the toast she had forgotten under the grill. Whenever the girls visited their various homes in the country they were sent back by their mothers laden with fresh vegetables and eggs as insurance against starvation, whether caused by penury, vanity or idleness. When these supplies ran low meals tended to become haphazard and skimped. Daphne was a tall, dark girl much given to fits of melancholy. She was constantly falling in love, and possessed feelings so fragile that they were easily wounded by heedless remarks made not only by her current swain but also by her flat-mates, who had to tread warily if they wished to avoid causing a fit of gloom to descend. She worked in an advertising agency. Her cousin Jane, the third member, was Caroline's school-friend. She had red hair, and with it an intolerant and fiery disposition. She usually wore spectacles, which she did not really need except for reading, but they accented her intense expression. Her judgement was shrewd and mature; and she had both the capacity for and the intention of going far in her career. She worked for a magazine syndicate and had already graduated from mere secretarial duties to proof-reading. She always moved about very rapidly, but was at the same time precise and neat and never clumsy. This morning she was also very hungry, and now urged Daphne to hurry with the breakfast.

'It's ready.'

Daphne, burdened with the tray, came into the large living-room that overlooked the square. She set it down on the table that stood in the window, covered with a gaily checked cloth. Jane's mother had provided that; it needed no ironing, and was washed, not nearly often enough, by anyone who was going to the launderette.

'Caro, hurry up. Breakfast's ready,' Jane called, snatching a piece of toast from the laden tray and beginning to gnaw it before Daphne had finished unloading.

Daphne glared at her.

'Ssh, you ass,' she hissed. 'She's not working this morning—probably wants to sleep.'

'Oh, I forgot.'

Jane sat down. She and Daphne worked regular office hours, and were still confused by Caroline's shift system. They never knew when to expect her back, and sometimes she herself was vague about her own duties. Unrepentant, Jane helped herself to more toast and spread it lavishly with butter.

'As a matter of fact, I think she is awake,' Daphne volunteered at last, relenting. 'I thought I heard her moving about.' Carefully, she poured out their coffee, spilling a little on the cloth in spite of her vigilance.

Before Jane could answer, Caroline entered the

room, sweeping in with a swirl of her long green dressing-gown. She beamed at them both and flung herself into a chair.

'I'm starving,' she said. 'Hi, everyone.'

'Hi,' replied the others absently, both busy cracking their eggs. Jane tapped hers neatly with a knife and decapitated it.

'Thought you'd sleep on today,' said Daphne through a mouthful of yolk and toast.

'I woke early,' said Caroline. She smiled down at her plate and played about with her egg-spoon.

Jane glanced sharply at her.

'You're up to something,' she remarked. 'What is it? You look thoroughly guilty; out with it.'

Caroline looked at her, grinning.

'Wouldn't you like to know?' she observed. 'I wonder what it could be!'

'Nick was here last night, wasn't he?' Jane said.

'Yes, but only for a few minutes.' Imperceptibly, Caroline's manner altered and became defensive. She had been working in the studios until eleven o'clock the night before; then Nicholas had brought her home, by which time the other two girls were in bed. They rarely cross-examined one another about their friends; but disapproval, if felt, was usually voiced, and opinions of candour rather than tact freely given.

'Well, Nick's all right,' Jane allowed. 'Not like that odious Gregory.'

68

'He was rather dim.' Caroline giggled. 'I can't imagine what I saw in him.' For a brief period Gregory, a bearded technician from the studios, had filled all her waking thoughts and much of her time; but now he had been replaced by Nick, who was so different, so right, and of whom even the intolerant Jane approved. She sat in a trance, her egg forgotten and the spoon suspended in mid-air, while she thought about him.

Jane and Daphne exchanged glances.

'Well, munch up, old dear,' Jane said, deciding her friend was too far advanced a case for further discussion at present. 'Your egg'll hatch at this rate. I'm off. 'Bye.'

She pushed back her chair, hurried out, and could presently be heard clattering in her room as she pulled drawers open and shut, finally banging the outer door of the flat behind her. Daphne, near the window, saw her walking quickly down the road opposite, pulling her raincoat on over her jersey and short, tight skirt as she went.

'What a rush she's always in,' said Caroline in a relaxed, dreamy voice. 'Poor old Jane, I wish she'd take things more slowly. She'll burn herself up going at such a pace.' She pushed her plate away and leaned back in her chair, holding her coffee cup in both hands as if it were a brandy goblet.

'She's doing all right,' said Daphne, beginning to pile up the crockery.

'I'll clear away, you leave it,' said Caroline benignly. 'I've hours of time.'

'Oh, thanks.' Daphne's rather heavy features softened. 'I ought to go, I suppose,' she said, making no effort to carry out this duty. She sighed heavily. 'I'm a bit like Jane, always hurrying too,' she added.

'Jane hurries because she can't help herself, even when she's got hours of time to spare. You hurry because you won't get started in time,' Caroline declared sagely, and sipped her coffee. 'Anyway, you've got oceans of time now, if I clear up. Relax. Calm down.' She set her cup back in place on the saucer and went on, 'Jane'll never get married if she stays so intense. Men like women to be relaxed.' She looked thoroughly relaxed herself as she said this. To Daphne her complacency was obvious.

'Oh, do they? Thanks for telling me,' she said bitterly. She was at the moment between romances, having considered herself put upon by her last love, Roger, who had soon taken for granted all the mending, ironing and cookery she had done in his service and ceased to be grateful, and she had not succeeded yet in finding a successor.

'Well, they do, you know,' said Caroline more gently. She felt sorry for Daphne, whose heart broke regularly three times a year. 'They hate fusses.'

'It's all very well for you, they swarm after you like bees after honey,' Daphne said, but with resignation, not envy now.

Caroline looked at her wistful expression and was filled with a desire to help her.

'You're too anxious, Daph,' she said. 'You plunge in, head first, just asking to be hurt. You try doing a bit of hurting yourself, instead.'

'I couldn't,' Daphne said. 'You see, it always matters so much, somehow. I never know if there will be anyone else.' She looked tragic.

'Oh, but there always is,' said Caroline bracingly.

'For you, yes.' Daphne looked from the fair, pink and white prettiness of the other girl to her own dark reflection in the mirror over the fireplace. Her image gazed mournfully back at her with large brown eyes. 'Not for me.'

'Oh, rubbish, Daph,' Caroline said firmly. 'How you love to wallow. You just need to cheer up and not mind too much, don't take every little thing to heart and brood on it. Maybe it will be next time lucky. Anyway, are you so keen to get married?'

'Isn't everyone?' Daphne asked. 'All, that is, except Jane. She never thinks about it, she just dreams of being editor.'

'She'll want to one day, when she meets someone who's just right, who'll make her forget all that,' said Caroline wisely. 'There's probably just one person only for her.' She sat, looking pensive, and Daphne felt a sudden affection for her as she realised, for the first time, that there was perception as well as warmth in her character.

'Everything's fine for you just now, Caro, isn't it?' she said, and she smiled, unable any longer to feel bitter.

Caroline nodded. 'I'm very happy and very lucky,' she said, serenely.

'You want to marry Nick?'

Another nod was the reply, and Daphne said: 'You will. I know it.' Then, to relieve the solemnity that was between them she laughed nervously and added: 'Jane and I will be bridesmaids.'

At this, Caroline sat up straight and looked grave.

'If you're not—if I don't ask you to be—' she paused, looking desperately embarrassed as she sought for words.

'Well?' Daphne, who had intended only to relax the tension of their conversation, showed dismay at her obvious failure.

'If I don't, it won't be because I don't want to, but for a very good reason,' burst out Caroline at last. 'You'll believe that, won't you?'

'Good heavens, yes.' Daphne was aghast at this reaction to her frivolous remark. Why on earth had she said it? How typically maladroit. 'I was only joking,' she said lamely.

'I know.' Caroline got up from the table. She made an effort to speak flippantly. 'It's just that one never knows what will happen. I might spring a surprise on you.'

'Yes. Well, maybe I'll beat you to the altar yet,' said Daphne carelessly. She walked across to the door. The brief harmony between them had ended, and it was she, as always, who had introduced the discord. 'I'll be late, I must dash,' she said, and left the room. She was always longer over her final preparations for the office than Jane, since she took more trouble over applying her lipstick and brushing her clothes, but soon she too was walking up the road to the bus-stop, dressed in a white plastic-leather coat and carrying a red umbrella.

Left alone, Caroline's mood of gaiety did not return. She stared out at the steadily falling rain, picking at the glass of the window-pane with a finger-nail. Her spirits drooped.

'Oh, hell, I can't help Daph and her moods,' she decided at last, and began to stack the breakfast things on the tray. She carried them out to the kitchen and washed up very noisily, breaking a cup in the process, and glaring down at the grimy water as she wielded her mop fiercely. 'What a thing to say,' she thought angrily. 'Trust Daph to put both feet right in, just like her. Oh, damn, damn, damn!'

She finished at last, and returned to the sitting-room. Still the rain streamed down, and she sat on the window-seat watching it fall while she thought of Jane and Daphne in their separate offices, the one eagerly over-efficient, the other so miserable and bewildered that her whole day would be blighted. In the end she could not avoid thinking about herself and her part in the silly squabble.

'It isn't any good, I'll have to ring up Daddy,' Caroline decided, as she, like the lowering sky, began to weep.

6

As Meriel drove away from the Grange she experienced a warm, internal glow that was not wholly due to the two cups of coffee she had drunk, or the rock cake she had nibbled. The sensation was due much more to a sense of satisfaction : Felicity, arriving simultaneously, had kissed her lightly and revealed that it was her birthday, so that throughout the morning she had basked in pleasant importance. She had decided to appear in the role of 'a good sport', and so had laughingly related how all her presents had been for use in the bathroom except for the mysterious gift with which Peter planned to surprise her this evening. She was allowed by the other women to retain the centre of the stage; around her sprang up an atmosphere of *bonhomie*, and soon a lively general conversation was in progress. The forthcoming Drama Group's production was discussed, and Meriel and Felicity, the only two members present, were congratulated on their courage in consenting to perform. All the rest promised to be in the audience.

Magnificent behind her large silver coffee-pot and

thermos jug of milk, Edith Browne gazed in a matri-
archal manner over her cashmere-covered bust at the
assembly and was pleased. She was much older than
any of her guests, and looked upon them all as she
had once been used to looking at the wives of lower
ranking officers, dragooning them for their good and
causing to meet those who never would from choice.
She acknowledged now, as then, no feuds and no anti-
pathies. She was well aware of the social prestige con-
ferred by her recognition and she used this knowledge
shrewdly when she wished to recruit helpers for the
various charitable projects round which she ran her
life now that the Army no longer claimed it. Today,
however, there was no ulterior motive for the gathering; it was purely social, and she was content with the
well-mannered semi-circle of local ladies ranged before
her. She allowed Meriel her spell of birthday glory,
and meanwhile spoke to all her guests in turn in a
regal way, enquiring about their families and gardens
and dispensing unasked-for advice upon both.

'All the same, she's a nice old girl,' Winifred observed as she followed Meriel to the car. 'She does a
lot of good with her fêtes and her jumbles.'

Meriel let the clutch in and the big car moved
slowly down the drive. Still it rained, and the wind-
screen wipers wagged frantically to and fro trying to
cope with the downpour. She could see in the mirror
Felicity following behind in her mini-car; her husband
drove the Bentley up to London every day.

'Yes,' Meriel said aloud. Privately, she was determining that when Lady Browne was forced by age or frailty (of which she as yet showed no sign), into retiring from leadership of the district, it would be she who assumed command. Others would be welcome as lieutenants in the field of welfare; Winifred for one, with her cooking and her herbs, would be very useful, but Meriel would reign supreme on the social pinnacle. 'Yes, she's wonderful,' Meriel repeated, hoping that her comment might one day reach its subject's ears.

'Rather her than me, chairman of all those worthy causes,' said Winifred, shivering inside her tweed coat. 'Phew, what a day.' She peered out at the depressing, sodden countryside. 'No sign of Rupert. Fancy riding in this wet, he must be keen.'

'Of course he is,' said Meriel. 'The heater will warm up in a minute.' She adjusted a lever and tepid air began to waft on to their knees. 'Nothing would keep him in,' she declared. 'And of course his pony must be exercised, wet or fine.' By now she had conveniently forgotten that Rupert had been most reluctant to carry out this duty; ostrich-like, she was able to remember only happy truths.

'What a nice boy he is,' said Winifred obligingly. 'Always so polite, and not rough or noisy like so many. How's Caroline?'

Meriel frowned, for here was another less pleasing reminder. She had managed successfully to banish the thought of Caroline's defection until now.

'Very busy, poor lamb,' she decided to say. 'She works much too hard, I'm afraid. I wish she'd give it up.'

'Oh well, everyone works now,' said Winifred mildly, 'and quite right too even if you and Peter can afford to keep her in idleness. How bored she'd be at home. All the young seem to be up in London. Doesn't she like her job? I thought it sounded very interesting.'

Meriel did not like being attacked, however indirectly.

'Oh yes, I think she does, but one has no idea who she's with,' she said. 'Such odd people seem to be working in the studios.'

'Oh, I don't know.' Winifred had lighted a cigarette and now opened the window for an instant to flick the ash outside, causing a flurry of damp air to enter the car. 'They must all be very clever, I should think it's great fun, fine experience.'

Meriel felt unable to cope with further argument; but she could not agree, so she drove faster and soon dropped Winifred back at her house. Five minutes later she was in her own drawing-room, where Hanni had made up the fire so that it blazed cheerfully, and where Felicity was already comfortably reclining on the sofa with a glass of sherry and the latest *Vogue*.

'I made myself at home,' she said lazily, putting down the magazine and stretching her slim body against the rust-coloured cushions. 'I poured yours out too, it's over there.'

Meriel sank down in a chair on the other side of the fireplace as though exhausted by the rigours of the morning.

'Thanks,' she said, and picked up the glass that stood on a small table by her side. 'I need this.' She sipped it, and then lighted a cigarette. 'Winifred was at her most earnest today,' she said.

Felicity shrugged. 'Poor old thing,' she said tolerantly. 'She's very worthy.'

'Boring to a degree,' said Meriel. 'She was on about Caroline, seemed to think her job's the tops.' Meriel's vocabulary was the despair of her son; she still relied upon schoolgirl expressions to make herself understood.

'She's been there some time now, hasn't she?' mused Felicity, who was interested in Caroline because she had always thought of her as so suitable for a future daughter-in-law. 'Are you going to let her stay?'

'She'll tire of it if we leave her,' said Meriel, who knew, though she would not admit it, that no words of hers would make Caroline do anything she had not already decided to do herself.

'She might be too stubborn to say she wants a change,' said Felicity.

'Not to me,' Meriel insisted. 'We could always save her pride somehow. She works such queer hours, I never know when to expect her home, not having regular weekends any more.'

'Gerald hasn't seen her for ages,' said Felicity. She swung round and sat up, her blued hair, puffed out round her thin, rather lined face, shining against the dark background of Meriel's curtains. 'He brought a girl down last weekend, in actual fact, not a bad little thing but she wasn't Caroline. I'd be sorry if anything went wrong.'

So would Meriel.

'We'll bring them together again,' she decided. 'I'll tell Caro she must come down next weekend—I'm sure she can change her duty if she really wants to, one always can.'

Felicity said nothing, but sipped her sherry and looked at her friend. Meriel might, by sheer refusal to give up a cherished idea, yet bring off something that she herself was beginning to think would not come to pass. Gerald had been very attentive to the rather plump young woman he had produced, and she had clearly thought him wonderful. Desperate measures might be needed. It was a pity Caroline had developed this independent streak.

There was a tap at the door and Hanni came into the room carrying an enormous cellophane-wrapped armful of carnations. Rain had saturated the cellophane, which was shrunken and specked as a result, and water dripped from the stalks of the flowers where Hanni had thrust them into a jug of water until Meriel returned.

'Hanni, take care! The carpet!' exclaimed Meriel.

Hanni merely took a cloth from her pocket and held it beneath the stems.

'I fetch a vase,' she said. 'You will arrange these now, Madame?'

'Oh, no, take them away, Hanni. I'll do them later,' Meriel said.

'Rupert fetched them,' said Hanni. 'They are for birthday wishes from all your family,' and she beamed. 'I take them to the kitchen now.'

She went away, and Meriel made a face of despair.

'Lucky you,' said Felicity.

Before Meriel could reply Hanni came back.

'Rupert isn't back yet from his riding. Would you wish for me to serve your lunch, Madame, and he perhaps has his with me in the kitchen? I fear for the chicken to be dry.'

'Oh, isn't he tiresome? I suppose he forgot his watch.' Meriel got up and pulled her jacket down. 'Very well, Hanni. We won't wait.'

'I take away his place, then all is prepared,' Hanni said, withdrawing.

'Thank you, Hanni. We'll come in a minute,' said Meriel. She picked up the sherry decanter and poured out a second glass for Felicity and for herself.

'Wretched boy, he loses all sense of time when he's on that pony,' she said, and Felicity believed her.

7

THE pony laid back its ears and glared at Rupert through mean little eyes. Determined not to expose the extent of his apprehension to the cause of it, the boy marched resolutely towards Martian, shaking the bowl of corn that he carried and calling optimistically.

'Martian, Martian, good boy, come up then.'

Martian had not the least intention of coming up. He allowed Rupert to approach almost close enough to touch the head-collar which he always wore since otherwise he would never be caught, and then retreated, still looking balefully at his pursuer. This went on for over fifteen minutes, during which Rupert grew increasingly wet and miserable and the pony more bad-tempered.

'I'll give up in five minutes,' Rupert decided, and would have done so if Mr. Hitchin, the farmer who owned Martian's field, had not arrived and taken Martian by surprise from the rear. Even so, the pony nipped his captor's arm and got a cuff on the muzzle for his pains.

'Oh, thanks awfully, Mr. Hitchin.' Rupert, with his

reprieve lost, tried not to sound ungrateful. 'I couldn't get near him.'

'Sly devil, isn't he?' remarked Mr. Hitchin, surrendering his grip on the pony's nose band as Rupert slipped his rope through it. 'Wants plenty of work, doesn't he? Ponies all do, I say.'

'Yes, you're right,' Rupert agreed politely.

Martian pushed him roughly, thrusting his nose into the bowl under the boy's arm and blowing into it as he munched the handful of corn in the bottom. When it was gone he consented to be led out of the field and over to the shed where Rupert kept his tack. Soon he was tied up securely while his reluctant owner tried to dry his back with straw and an old towel before saddling him. At last he was ready, the girths pulled as tight as Martian, blowing himself out to inflate his belly, would allow, and the bridle on. The pony moved off sideways while Rupert was swinging himself into the saddle.

'Damn you, stand still,' Rupert growled, and, surprised at his angry voice, Martian obeyed for a moment. Eventually, and this time at Rupert's decree and not the pony's, they moved away. Hanni came out of the kitchen with a lump of sugar for the undeserving Martian and a toffee for Rupert, who began to feel more cheerful as he rode down the drive with the pony briefly subdued as he crunched the sugar under his bit.

Outside the gate the shelter of the trees ended, and as the pair went down the road the wind and the driving rain caught them gustily. Martian skirmished, head down, turning his tail to the wind. Rupert pulled him round, shortening his already short reins and digging his knees into the saddle.

'Cut it out, Martian,' he commanded. 'Come along, let's trot on.'

They set off up the road at a brisk pace, the pony leaning heavily on the bit and every now and then breaking into an excited canter. Rupert checked him, trying to keep his head up; the exercise soon began to make him feel warmer, but the rain found its way down his neck in spite of his upturned collar, and when he bent forward it streamed from the peak of his velvet cap past his nose. He had forgotten his gloves and the reins were slippery in his wet hands. A few cars passed, sending cascades of water from their wheels against Martian's legs. He shied violently at a bus, for the red double-deckers were one of his many aversions, and Rupert, slightly off balance, lost the rhythm of the trot for a few paces. At last, however, Martian's flow of energy diminished and he began to go more steadily until Rupert pulled him back into a walk to let them both rest. Because of the weather and the impetuousness of the pony it was impossible for Rupert to think of anything except his present circumstances and the job in hand. His horizon was limited to the feel of the strong muscles under him and the view of the short, thick neck and small twitching ears in front. He did not immediately recognise his mother's car as it went by, and only raised a hand in vague salute after it had gone, too late to be observed.

Coming to the crossroads, Rupert decided to go over the common. Martian was settling down now, and he could have a good canter over the heather. It would stretch him well, so that they could soon go home. He turned off the road and trotted down a rutted path between treelined banks. When the going improved Rupert eased his hold on the pony and let him canter.

When Martian behaved, Rupert enjoyed his rides. He liked the feeling of freedom and the occasional moments when he felt skilled and in control, but the pony's temperament was so uncertain that he never knew what tricks to expect. Sometimes Martian showed his power by bucking; sometimes he became obstinate and refused to go where Rupert wanted him to; sometimes he developed panic fears of stones, shrubs or other harmless landmarks; occasionally, for lack of other inspiration, he simply put his head down and went. Today, after a time, sensing that he was headed towards home, he did this again. Extended like a miniature racehorse he tore along, pounding through mud and puddles and under the boughs of overhanging trees. Rupert sawed vainly at the reins, but the pony simply leaned further on the bit and went even faster. Forced to duck so that his head would not be struck by branches, Rupert peered ahead between the pony's ears looking for hazards in their path and trying to steer some sort of a course that would save them both from coming to grief. He was terrified, but too numb to be aware of the depth of his fear.

At last, after what seemed like several miles, Martian began to tire. Rupert, sick with relief, hauled up his head.

'You devil,' he gasped, longing to thrash the animal but lacking the nerve, for Martian would only buck violently if he did. 'I'm damned if I'll take you home now, you'll jolly well go on till you drop, then perhaps you'll behave tomorrow,' he said, turning the pony firmly away so that his tail pointed towards home. Rupert would not let him rest but made him trot on. I must master him, he thought, knowing that if only he could always do this Martian might become quite well behaved. He knows I'm scared of him, Rupert admitted to himself. Well, at least he was not now at the Pony Club having his shame witnessed by dozens of competent little girls whose average age was ten and who seemed born to the saddle. Grimly he drove the pony on, keeping him on a tight rein and at a fast trot. They went down tracks and paths and across an open stretch of gorse-strewn common. Rupert's own back ached long before Martian showed signs of having had enough. At last they came to the edge of the common and clattered down on to a lane. Rupert let the pony walk. He shook back the sleeve of his mackintosh and looked at his watch: it said ten o'clock.

That must be wrong; it had been about ten when he left home. He put it to his ear and shook it, but what with the noise of the wind and the rain and the sound of Martian's shoes on the tarmac he could not hear whether or not it was going. He sighed and gave up, deciding it was probably about half-past eleven. There was an old, soft fruit-drop in his pocket, and he took it out, holding an end of the grubby paper between his teeth so that he could unwrap it with a pull of his fingers. He sucked it with satisfaction. Martian walked demurely along, at last, it seemed, subdued, and Rupert relaxed. He was almost enjoying himself when with a roar as its gears changed another bus came by. It passed quite slowly, went on up the road a little way and then stopped to let a passenger get off. Martian, taken by surprise, shied as its hated red sides drew level, and Rupert fell over his head. He landed heavily, striking his shoulder on the road, and Martian trotted off in the wake of the now departing bus.

Slowly, Rupert got to his feet. His arm hurt and he felt jarred all over, but he was more troubled by humiliation at having come off in such a manner. Whoever said it took seven falls to make a horseman ought to be shot, he thought ruefully. He'd come off many more times than that himself and now had done it again through being caught napping. This time it looked as if he would have to walk home, too, as Martian was disappearing. He trudged after him despairingly, rubbing his arm, and wondering if it was too much to hope that Martian might vanish for ever. It was. The pony stopped and began cropping the grass at the side of the road. The reins had fallen forward round his ears and as he moved one foreleg became entangled with them, so that he was hobbled. Rupert was able to catch him very easily, though Martian was not co-operative about having his feet lifted free of the reins.

'Oh, well done,' said a voice.

Rupert jumped, startled at finding that he was not alone in his plight. A short woman who seemed enormously stout was hurrying up to him from the other side of the pony. Unruly hair escaped from a scarf tied over her head and her drab raincoat was stretched across her body. Rupert realised slowly that she was not fat, but pregnant. 'The bus frightened him, didn't it?' the woman was saying.

'Yes.'

'Bad luck.' She looked at him, trying not to seem anxious. His face was streaked with mud; between splashes it also seemed pale.

'I shouldn't have come off,' said Rupert.

'Oh well, everyone does,' said the woman cheerfully. 'Hurt yourself? Road's hard, isn't it?'

'Yes, it is,' Rupert laughed shakily. 'I'm all right, though, thanks. Banged my arm a bit, that's all.'

'Well, come along to my house and have a wash,' said the woman. 'I live just up here. I'm sure you've had a bit of a shake-up. Or do you live close by?'

'Oh no, miles away, at Merelands in Timpsley,' said Rupert. He began to walk slowly along beside the woman, Martian meekly accompanying them with his head drooping abjectly in the rain as though penitent.

'Oh, then you must be Rupert Graham,' said the woman, looking at him with new interest. She had been trying to decide whether her duty lay in urging him back on to his pony without delay to ensure the restoration of his nerve, or in making sure that he was in fact uninjured; he did seem pale, and a wash would reveal how much was due to shock.

'Yes, I am,' Rupert said, surprised at being recognised by his address. 'I expect you know my mother?' he said politely, yet feeling obscurely that this plain and shabby woman would somehow not be one of his mother's friends.

'My husband knows your father. They catch the same train to London every day,' she said. 'Come along, Rupert. This is where I live.'

They had reached a rambling old house set back from the road behind a crumbling wall.

'What a lovely house,' said Rupert, staring at it.

'Yes, it is nice,' said his new friend. 'I'm glad you like it. It's one of the old village houses that were here long before the commuters arrived.'

They turned into the gateway. A laden shopping basket stood in the drive where it had been hastily abandoned while its owner hurried to Rupert's rescue.

'This is kind of you,' Rupert said. 'I would be glad of a wash.'

'I'm glad I was here,' said the good samaritan briskly. 'We'll put the pony in the garage, he won't get out of there.'

'Won't he damage things?' Rupert suggested doubtfully.

To his surprise Martian consented to enter the dark garage without objecting.

'There's not much here,' said his hostess. 'We've another shed full of ruck. Let's tie him up.'

She found an end of line lying on a shelf and gave it to Rupert.

'Use this,' she said. 'We don't want your bridle broken, he might tear the reins.'

Rupert threaded the line through the bridle, wincing slightly as he caught his sore arm. The woman helped him, and they secured the end to a bolt in the wall. Martian was left a prisoner.

'There, that's all right. Now come along,' said the woman.

Rupert said, 'Your basket,' and went off down the drive again to fetch it for her. She saw him put his right hand down to pick it up and then quickly turn so that he used his left instead. He came back, looking slightly embarrassed.

'Thank you, Rupert,' said the woman, and he carried it to the house.

They went through the back door, and she made

him take off his wet mackintosh. He made a face as he pulled it away from his right arm.

'That arm does hurt you, doesn't it?' she said. 'Can you move it properly?'

He lifted it with difficulty, and could not raise it over his head.

'If you landed on it I expect you've bruised it,' said the woman. She thought that it could not be broken; if he had fractured it he would not be able to move it at all.

It was warm in the kitchen. When Rupert returned there after washing his face and hands his hostess had removed her scarf and raincoat and was busy at the stove.

'I thought some hot soup would be nice,' she said. 'Sit down, Rupert.'

Obediently he pulled out a chair from the table and sat down. The mug of steaming Bovril she gave him soon made him feel better and a little colour returned to his face. She sat opposite him with another mug for herself.

'I ought to have taken Martian's saddle off,' Rupert began to worry.

'Oh, he won't hurt for a while,' said the woman. 'He might have got chilled if you had. Do you ride every day?'

Suddenly Rupert found that he was telling her that everyone thought he loved riding when really he hated it because he was afraid, and he felt no shame as he looked at the kind face watching him with concern.

'Lots of things that are fun are frightening,' she said. 'Motor-racing, mountain-climbing, and so on.'

'Yes, but you don't have to do them unless you want to,' said Rupert. 'No one makes you. And there isn't another being, like a pony with an obstinate nature, to struggle with.'

'I think you should talk to your father,' said the woman quietly. A change of pony to one with some sense and the fine nature which she knew horses were capable of possessing was probably all that was needed.

'Well, you see, my mother thinks I like it, and anyway she wants me to do it,' Rupert said. 'I don't have to ride at school.'

'Well, tell your father if you can,' said the woman. 'Now, I think you'd better ring your mother up. She'll be wondering where you are. It's half-past twelve. Perhaps you'd like to stay and have lunch with me? It may stop raining by this afternoon.'

'It's very kind of you,' said Rupert, 'but it's my mother's birthday and I must get back. No one will worry if I'm late, though. Hanni, that's our cook, knew I might be because mother's having someone to lunch.'

This was an obscure explanation, but he obviously felt he ought to go. He looked better now, and perhaps it would be just as well if he did get back on to his bad-tempered pony without too long an interval. She helped him into his mackintosh again and went out with him to the garage.

'Come and see me if you're riding this way again, Rupert,' she said when he had mounted and Martian was standing like a model pony waiting for the signal to move off. 'I'm nearly always here except on Tuesday and Friday mornings when I shop regularly. Call in for elevenses.'

'I'd love to,' Rupert said. 'Thanks awfully.' He raised his cap with his left hand, holding the reins a little awkwardly as he bent forward over his other arm. 'Goodbye,' he said.

She watched him go, and stood in the gateway till he was out of sight with the pony trotting briskly again but perfectly well behaved. She felt there was no point in worrying his mother by telephoning now; she would wait till he had had time to reach home and then she would ring up to make sure he had arrived safely. Slowly, heavily, Stella Wheeler walked back to the house.

8

I⊤ was stuffy in the office. The air, stale and enervating, made Joan feel stupid as well as depressed. She had pulled her window open and then had to close it all but a crack because the rain had come eddying in and had never ceased to fall. As she typed, a cup of tea, forgotten, had cooled beside her, with a scum from too much milk congealing on the surface. She reached the end of a page, ripped it out of her typewriter and clipped it to a bundle of papers. After she had added these to a pile already waiting in a wire basket she pushed back her chair and stretched, sighing, then rubbed her eyes. The day would be a hard one all round. In addition to the pile of work on hand, Peter, who was spending the morning in Court, had charged her with the task of buying a poodle for Meriel. She had listened patiently while he described how he had forgotten the date and what he had said at home, smothering the resentment she felt at being asked to do this particular thing. He had asked her if she could think of a better idea, and when she could not, she meekly agreed to track a poodle down. She had telephoned to one or two kennels that were listed in

94

the trades directory and was going to see some puppies, but the whole expedition filled her with reluctance. She was sure she would not be back in time to lunch with Peter; she would lose her chance of telling him her decision and it would be weeks before she would be able to muster the determination to do it again. In any case, even if she got to Bellini's in time, how could she say such a thing today? She would have to wait till the excitement of Meriel's birthday had died down. Once more she sighed. In spite of the distractions she must keep to her resolve; Peter would have to learn to run his own errands or train her successor. Her youth had slipped away from her while she existed on the fragments of his life that were all he could give her; if she was ever to break away and find another way to live she must do it soon.

There was a loud knock on her door and it burst open. Joan looked up, startled into anger by the abrupt intrusion. When she saw Caroline standing in the doorway she could only stare in surprise.

'Joan, hullo.' Caroline came into the room and closed the door behind her. Her yellow poplin raincoat shone with wet, and she had a plastic bonnet tied over her hair. This she now removed as she crossed the floor towards Joan's desk.

Joan got up. It was not unknown for Caroline to come to the office, but today she was obviously here for some urgent reason. The way she almost ran and her breathless voice revealed her to be under some considerable stress.

'Well, Caroline, what a surprise,' said Joan. 'Here, let me take your coat, it's soaked.'

'I can't stop, I'm in a fearful rush,' Caroline said. 'Where's Daddy? He isn't in his office.'

'He's in Court,' said Joan. 'He'll be back this afternoon. What's the matter? Can I help?'

Caroline leaned over the desk.

'But he must be here, I've got to see him,' she cried. 'This afternoon'll be too late.'

'Can't you tell me what's wrong?' Joan said again.

'Oh, nothing's wrong,' Caroline answered. 'Oh well, I suppose it is in a way. I wasn't going to say anything to anyone until afterwards, and then I realised I'd have to tell Daddy.' And she began to weep. 'Daddy must come,' she wailed.

'Come where? Now sit down, Caroline, and try to tell me,' said Joan in the manner of a calm nurse. She pushed the girl gently into a chair. 'If you're really in trouble I can get a message to your father.'

'It's not trouble.' Caroline blew her nose and stopped crying to laugh in a somewhat hysterical way. 'I'm really very happy. I'm getting married today.'

'Caroline!' Joan gaped at her.

'Oh, don't look so shocked, Joan.' Caroline began to giggle. 'It's all right, honestly, I'm not in that sort of trouble.'

'I should hope not,' said Joan primly, and then

more realistically, 'Caroline, you do mean what you've just said?'

'Oh, I mean it,' said Caroline. 'I'm being married at half-past two at St. Mary's, and I want Daddy to come.'

Joan was beginning to catch up. She took a deep breath and looked steadily at Caroline, who began to wear a slightly rebellious expression.

'Your father and mother don't know about this.' It was a statement, not a question.

'No, they don't. Nick and I decided it was the only way,' said Caroline defensively. 'Well, I did really. Nick wanted to tell them and so on, but I knew what a ghastly fuss Mother would make so I made him give in. And then this morning I suddenly realised I couldn't do it without Daddy knowing.'

Joan did not know what to say. It was not for her to preach, nor would it help the situation to grow angry.

'You've met Nick, don't you remember?' Caroline was saying. 'He was at our party that you came to.'

'Yes, I remember him,' Joan said. She had been touched when Caroline had impulsively asked her to a party that the three girls had given in their flat, and she had a clear picture in her mind of the very tall, dark young man whom she had noticed like a limpet at Caroline's side most of the evening. 'I thought he was very nice,' she said truthfully. 'But Caroline, my dear, this is a cruel thing to do to your parents, rushing to marry so secretively.'

'We aren't rushing, Joan,' said Caroline. 'We've thought about it for ages. But you don't know Mother. She'd have first of all made a terrible fuss because I'm not marrying Gerald Manners, who she's had lined up for me for years, not that he's the least bit interested in me any more than me in him. And then, if she'd accepted that I wouldn't marry Gerald she'd make a fearful row about Nick being a television producer and not a stockbroker or belted earl or other social or money catch. Then, even if she got used to that idea, she'd make us have the most awful elaborate do at St. Margaret's or somewhere, with rows of bridesmaids and poor Nick having everyone staring at the back of his neck, and Mother in red velvet or something equally grisly busy acting the part of the bride's mother for all she was worth. No, thank you!'

Joan was silent while the room seemed to echo Caroline's outburst. Then she said, 'I must say, I sympathise with your feelings about big weddings, Caroline. But you could have got married quietly at Timpsley, surely, with just your families?'

'Nick hasn't any family, only a brother,' said Caroline. 'And anyway, Mother wouldn't have let it be quiet. She'd have seized the chance to cut a dash.'

'Well, you may be right,' Joan said. 'I hardly know your mother. But she's sure to be very hurt. Why don't you ring her up? There's time for her to catch a train and be there. She couldn't spoil it now.'

'No,' Caroline said. 'She could. She could create an atmosphere.'

Joan gave up. 'Well, my dear, I haven't said any of the right things,' she said. 'I hope you'll be very happy, and your Nick is a very lucky young man.' She put an arm round the girl's shoulders, and Caroline, to her astonishment, suddenly hugged her and kissed her warmly.

'Dear old Joan. What on earth would Daddy do without you?' she said emotionally. 'Poor you.'

Joan stiffened.

'It must be awful, wearing your life away in faithful devotion with no rewards,' Caroline went on. 'Never any hope of everything coming right. Well, maybe it will one day.'

'I don't know what you're talking about,' said Joan stiffly. 'I've appreciated all the years I've worked for your father.'

Caroline let her go and stood back, looking at her.

'And he has appreciated you,' she said solemnly. 'At least he's had something,' and then, as the tell-tale colour sprang into Joan's face she turned away. 'Now how can we get Daddy?' she asked.

Joan busied herself with some papers at the desk.

'St. Mary's, at two-thirty,' she said, writing it down while she tried to speak normally. 'I'll make sure he knows. And what about your lunch. Where are you having it?'

'At the flat, I suppose,' said Caroline. 'I've got to

finish packing. Nick wanted to take me out to lunch but at least, you'll be glad to hear, I've stuck to convention enough not to let him.'

'Your father always lunches at Bellini's on Wednesdays,' said Joan. 'He'll be there about a quarter to one. Do you know where it is? In Diego Street?'

'Yes, I know it.' Caroline was watching her steadily.

'You go there and have lunch with him. I'll get a message to him meanwhile, but I've got to go and buy a poodle.'

'Buy a poodle?' Caroline stared.

'Yes. It's your mother's birthday,' Joan said, not enlarging upon the fact. But Caroline realised what had happened.

'She'll love it, of course. It's just what she lacks,' she said. 'So he forgot at last.'

'Your father's been very busy,' said Joan.

'So because of the poodle you'll be missing your Wednesday lunch with Daddy,' said Caroline slowly.

'Yes.' Joan choked on the word, realising as she uttered it the admission it made.

'Well, I think it's all bloody,' said Caroline. 'For you and Daddy, I mean. But thanks, Joan. I'll go to Bellini's.' She stood up, tall and beautiful. 'I absolutely must dash. I trust you to deal with Daddy and come to the wedding too, poodle and all, if you can,' she said, and was gone.

Left alone, Joan sank into her chair and hid her face in her hands. She felt utterly battered. She did not know which direction to let her thoughts take. Peter would be stunned by the news of his daughter's wedding. She decided to call round at the Courts herself before going off to the kennels. It would be too difficult to put Caroline's case over in a note if she were to send one by messenger. She tried to thrust into the back of her mind the disquieting revelation that Caroline seemed to understand the position between her father and herself.

9

THE Judge in his scarlet robes gazed impartially down at the half-filled court, peering with small brown eyes like nuts beneath shaggy brows below his wig. Peter and his clerk made notes as their client, in answer to counsel, slowly revealed the history of twelve years of miserable marriage. Witnesses swore to his wife's infidelities and very soon the decree was granted. Wearily the petitioner, a shabby, tired man, left the court and Peter followed. He handled very few divorce cases, but where a client for whom he did a lot of other business became involved he took on the case if asked. This man was a director of a small company who brought a lot of work to Peter's firm, and now they had helped him through these drab proceedings. Peter followed the stocky figure wondering why such a decent, honest man should be brought so low. And how shabby, how degraded too am I, Peter reflected as they passed through doors into the corridor. He spoke a few cheering words to his client who then hurried away, eager to leave the ancient building which might well be haunted by the ghosts of long-defunct barristers and litigants.

Joan rose from a bench where she had been waiting while the case was in progress. In spite of his thoughts, Peter's face lightened with pleasure when he saw her.

'All right?' she asked.

He nodded and said, 'What's up? Trouble?' He knew something unusual must have happened to bring her here. Then he remembered the poodle. 'Couldn't you get it?'

'I'm just going to see some,' she said. 'That's all under control, and I've ordered a collar too, a red one. It will be ready this afternoon with the label inscribed. And I got a licence.'

'Oh, well done,' he said. 'What is it, then?'

'I can't tell you here. Can't we go?' Joan said, glancing round at the gowned figures who stalked the corridor.

'What about our lunch?' said Peter as they walked away down the stairs and out into hall.

'I won't make it today,' she replied. 'I shan't be back in time from getting the dog. But you must go to Bellini's, Peter. Caroline's expecting to meet you there. She's just been round to the office.'

'Caroline?' Peter looked astounded. 'I telephoned her this morning and there was no reply from the flat. I thought she must be out somewhere. She forgot her mother's birthday.'

'She must have been on her way to see you when you rang her,' Joan said. 'I'm not surprised she forgot her mother's birthday.'

'Oh, why? What do you mean?'

Joan thought, here goes.

'She's getting married this afternoon. She wants you to give her away.'

Peter stood still, at last jolted completely out of his routine way of thinking. Joan hurried on into the same explanations that she had listened to from Caroline earlier. She glossed over the reactions that had been anticipated from Meriel, but Peter filled in the gaps.

'Caro's right. Meriel would have wanted all the fandango,' he said. 'But what I can't understand is why Caro didn't. This is almost as if she were ashamed, slinking off.'

'I think I understand,' Joan said. 'And that's why you can be happy about it.' She had had time for thinking it out as she drove in the taxi to find him. 'At her age most girls do want the trimmings, they want to cut a dash themselves. But she doesn't want her Nick exposed—bridegrooms always seem so defenceless. And she won't risk anything harming whatever exists between them both. Young plants bruise easily, Peter.' She looked at him. Older ones recovered more quickly from a bad crushing and grew even stronger, she thought. 'You'll meet her, Peter, won't you. And be kind,' she pleaded, as though she had ever known him be anything else.

'Yes. Yes of course.' Peter was thinking. 'What have I got this afternoon? Anything urgent?'

'Nothing as vital as this,' said Joan. 'I'll ring up old

Mr. Parkinson, you'd got him at three, and say you've had an important call. Goodness knows, it's true.'

'Bless you.' Peter patted her arm absently 'Meriel will take it hard,' he said. 'However will she explain to her friends?'

Joan did not care. That was not her problem. 'She'll think of something,' she said. 'You'll find you can cope. It's too late to get them to change their plans.'

'I suppose so. Anyway, I think they're right, this is the best idea,' said Peter. 'Awful though it is. Meriel would have taken charge of the whole business, even their feelings, leaving them nothing.' He looked sadly at Joan.

'Yes, well don't worry, I'm sure they've as much chance of being happy as most people,' Joan said. Peter looked forlorn and she longed to help him in spite of the jealous misery which was the chief emotion that nowadays she experienced. 'I must get off to those kennels,' she said. 'The woman will think I'm never coming.' She resolved to buy the first poodle she saw and let Meriel think herself lucky.

But Peter was travelling on in his thoughts.

'Rupert will be upset,' he said.

'Oh, I don't know,' said Joan bracingly. 'He's young enough to pass it over. Now I must go. Don't be late, the child will be terrified of what you'll say.'

'I won't be angry,' Peter said. 'But I can hardly take it in.' He twiddled his umbrella. 'I wish you'd come to the wedding too,' he said.

'Caroline asked me,' she could not resist saying. At least they had both wanted her then, while Meriel, the mother, was left outside.

'Come if you're back in time,' Peter said. 'And to hell with the office.'

'I'll try,' said Joan.

He watched her go hurrying away and followed her more slowly. Clandestine though it might be, and shameful, at least there was warmth and life in their relationship. He found a taxi quickly and was soon at Bellini's waiting for his daughter.

To Caroline, hurrying to meet him and apprehensive, he looked suddenly old. With the heightened perception being in love had brought her, she noticed the lines on his face, the slight retreat of his hair and the thickening of his body. She felt a wave of affection for him and clung to him when he kissed her as she had done when she was a little girl.

'Well, well, Caro,' he said, smiling hard to show that she was not in disgrace.

'You know? Joan told you?' she asked anxiously.

'Yes, she did.' Peter beamed. 'Now a drink, Caro. What's it to be? Champagne for the bride?'

'No thanks, I hate it,' Caroline shuddered. 'And it'd be awful to arrive tiddly. Just some sherry, please. And we must be quick.'

'We will be,' Peter said. He ordered their drinks, and while they waited there was a little silence between them. Each was conscious of the drama of the moment.

'Are you furious?' she asked at last.

'No,' Peter said. 'I hope I understand, Caro. Maybe you could have found a way of hurting your mother less without altering your plans, but I don't know. Anyway, it's too late now, isn't it? I mean, you do intend to marry this chap?'

'Oh, Daddy, yes,' she said, very gravely. 'Nick was awfully against it being a secret,' she went on. 'You must believe that, Daddy. He went all old-fashioned and said he ought to come and ask you for my hand and tell you his prospects. He earns quite a lot, we'll easily manage. You needn't think I'll starve.'

'Good, my dear,' said Peter. 'He sounds the right sort of fellow. I'll like him, won't I?'

'Oh, of course you will.' She giggled, and went on to spend most their time together telling him about Nicholas. When she paused for breath, he said, 'Did you forget that it's Mummy's birthday today?'

'Oh, heavens, how awful! I did,' she gasped. 'What can we do?'

'I've fixed flowers from us all,' said Peter, knowing that by now Rupert would have carried out his mission.

'Oh, well done,' said Caroline. 'Of course, it's always so important to her. And I know, I've had a brainwave. We're crossing to France tonight, with the car, we're going to drive right across Europe to Italy. Won't it be bliss? We'll call at home on the way, it won't take much longer to go round by Timpsley. We'll take a huge box of chocs. How's that for a scheme? It'll be harder to confess in person than by letter, of course, but if we load her with birthday wishes Mother won't be able to gloom on and be cross.'

Peter was not so sure, but the idea had possibilities and was worth a try. At least it would lessen Meriel's feeling of having been forgotten, and if they thought her worth calling on as they set off for their honeymoon she could not feel slighted. He could already hear her telling Felicity, 'Poor darlings, such a funny idea to slip off as they did, but I was the first to be told.' He would also be reprieved from the difficult interview he had foreseen for himself. He would return to Merelands soon after Caroline and Nicholas left and continue the work of healing.

'And that way we can explain that you didn't know either till today, so she won't accuse you of conspiring with us,' Caroline said.

Peter had already decided that Meriel would convict him of duplicity. Perhaps, though, there was hope.

'Attack's the best method of defence,' Caroline told him.

'Very well, dear. You do whatever you like. Nicholas may have an opinion too,' he said.

'Poor Nick, he'll die of fright, but he'll think I'm

right,' said Caroline. 'He likes having everything open and aboveboard.'

'Quite right,' said Peter. 'Good for Nick.' He felt suddenly very old and used, but as he looked at his daughter's shining eyes he thought that Nicholas would be well rewarded for his courage.

10

AT two o'clock, when it was time for Meriel and Felicity to leave if they were not to be late at their Drama Group's meeting, Rupert was still not back from his ride and Hanni expressed anxiety.

'Oh, he's probably gone further than he intended and forgotten the time,' said Meriel impatiently. 'He'll come presently.' She swept out, leaving Hanni disconsolately looking at the closed oven door behind which Rupert's chicken and vegetables were slowly congealing.

The rain had slackened and now only a fine drizzle was falling. The garden wore an aura of dejection; everything drooped under the mantle of water. Hanni grimaced at the dismal outdoor scene and thought wistfully of her native mountains where the air was fresh and sweet. She comforted herself by surveying her bright, clean kitchen, where all was cheerful and it was warm. She gave the boiler a riddle for luck, then glanced at the electric clock on the wall: ten past two, and still no Rupert. She sighed, and rearranged the place she had laid for him at the kitchen table, adding a bottle of Coca Cola, which he loved, to the collection of cutlery, butter, cheese and celery which waited for him. Still he did not come.

Hanni went into the drawing-room and tidied it, shaking up the cushions and putting away the sherry decanter. Two large ashtrays were filled with lipsticked stubs, and she emptied them into the fire before she built that up with logs and little lumps of coal to last through the afternoon. Rupert, when he returned, would want to spread himself out on the sofa and read, she thought indulgently. After being out for so long in the rain he would need and deserve a rest in the warmth. She sat down herself for a few minutes and skimmed through *The Daily Mail* that lay on the pouffe before the hearth. When the telephone bell rang, shattering the silence, she started guiltily at the interruption and hastily folded up the newspaper before she answered.

'Hullo, Timpsley 659,' she recited, as Meriel had taught her.

'Is that Mrs. Graham?' asked a woman's voice.

'No, she is out. I take a message, please?' Hanni said.

'I rang to ask if Rupert had got back all right,' said the voice.

'Rupert is not here,' Hanni said.

'Who is that speaking?' The voice was firmer now.

'It is Hanni, the maid, who speaks,' came the lyrical reply.

'Oh. Well, has Rupert come home?' asked the caller.

'He is riding. He is not come back yet,' Hanni said.

'You mean he has not yet come home from his ride?' The voice, urgent now, spoke very slowly and clearly.

'No. I expect him all the time. His lunch grows cold,' Hanni said. 'Who is this, please?'

'It's Mrs. Wheeler. I met Rupert this morning, he had a fall from his pony and came to my house to wash and rest. He left at about half-past twelve. He should have reached home an hour ago.' Stella's voice was anxious.

'Oh heaven!' exclaimed Hanni, staring frantically round the room as though Rupert might materialise from the atmosphere.

Stella realised that Hanni might, in her continental way, become over-emotional. She said: 'Are you alone in the house? Do you know where Mrs. Graham is?'

'She has gone to a meeting. I know not what,' Hanni said.

'Do you know where?' demanded Stella.

'No, but Mrs. Manners went with her. Perhaps at the home of Mrs. Manners they will know,' said Hanni, displaying great common sense.

Stella decided not to entrust the query to Hanni, practical though she seemed to be.

'I'll ring up Mrs. Manners' house and find out,' she

said. 'I'll ring you back afterwards to see if he has returned meanwhile.'

'I go to look in the field if the pony is there. Then I come back and wait by the telephone,' Hanni said, responding to the authority in the voice at the other end of the line.

'Very well. I'll telephone again in ten minutes,' said Stella. She rang off, and began to search in the directory for the number of the Manners' house. Hanni, pausing only to drape a mackintosh taken at random from the collection hanging in the cloakroom round her shoulders, ran out into the garden and down to the field. The gate stood open, and there was no sign of Martian. She hurried back to the house, and before entering it again went down the drive to the gate, where she gazed up and down the road, but there was no one in sight, and no sound of hooves upon the road. Quickly she returned to the drawing-room, and stood by the telephone, shifting her weight nervously from one foot to the other while she waited for the bell to ring. When at last it did, and she lifted the receiver, she nearly knocked the whole instrument off its table in her agitation.

'Yes? Mrs. Wheeler?' she gasped.

'Hanni, there's no reply from Mrs. Manners' house.' Stella's voice was deliberately calm. 'I think, as we don't know how to get hold of Mrs. Graham, that we should tell the police Rupert is missing.' While she listened to the telephone bell ringing unanswered in the Manners' house, she had come to this decision. 'I suppose he isn't back?'

'No, madame, and I have looked along the road and he is not to be seen. Shall I perhaps go and search for him?' Hanni was eager to take action of some sort.

'No, you must stay where you are in case he comes.' Stella hoped events would prove her to be needlessly alarmist, but if a child of her own were missing she knew what she would want done. 'Telephone me at once if he does get back,' she said. 'Timpsley Green 493. I will get in touch with the police now and explain.'

'Was Rupert hurt much when he fell?' Hanni demanded.

'No, not really. He seemed to be shaken up a bit, and he'd bruised his arm, but he appeared to be quite well enough to ride home.' Stella was not yet able to face the thought that she should not have allowed him to leave.

'Martian, he is not a kind pony,' Hanni said. 'I do not trust him, that one.'

'Well, don't worry too much, Hanni,' Stella said. 'He's probably just taking it slowly. I'll get on to the police now, they'll soon find him if he is. You'll stay there, won't you?' She had no idea what sort of girl Hanni was, but the breathless voice and the remark about Martian's character convinced her that she had Rupert's welfare at heart.

'Indeed yes! Oh, I do hope nothing has happened,' Hanni cried. 'I will not move until he comes.'

'It might be wise to put a hot-water bottle in his bed and see that his room is warm,' Stella suggested. 'Just in case he is hurt.' She thought too that it would be as well for Hanni to be employed while she waited, even though it was to be hoped such preparations would not be needed, rather than to sit wringing her hands beside the telephone.

'I will see to it,' Hanni promised.

'Right. I'll ring off now, Hanni,' Stella said.

The line went dead. Hanni replaced the receiver and walked slowly across the room to the window. Outside, the drizzle continued to fall and the sky was dark. In spite of her misgivings when Rupert was late home she had not really believed that he had met with any disaster. It was dreadful to realise that after all he might be hurt. She pictured a stretcher slung between two men in uniform, with Rupert's body inert upon it under a blanket, and shuddered.

That would not do. She shook herself and hurried out to put the heater on in his bedroom and boil a kettle for his hot-water bottle.

Half an hour later a police car drew up outside the house. A sergeant and a constable got out, and Hanni had opened the front door before they reached the step.

'You have found him?' she cried.

'Not yet, miss, but he can't be far away,' said the

sergeant, the shorter of the two. He spoke calmly, taking his notebook out of his breast pocket. The constable, young and fair, looked appreciatively at Hanni's pretty round face and large blue eyes as he stood a pace to the rear with his hands clasped behind his back. 'We just want to check one or two points with you. Mrs. Wheeler's given us the facts as she knows them, but maybe you can add a few details,' went on the sergeant.

'Oh, yes. Please come in.' Hanni stood aside and let them into the house. They stood in the hall while she answered the sergeant's questions, confirming what Stella had said and adding details of Rupert's clothes and general description. The police car had not passed him on its way to Merelands from Timpsley Green, which pointed to the fact that he must have taken a cross-country route home from there. Hanni could not guess which way he was most likely to have gone; there was a choice of several tracks over the common, and he might have chosen any of them.

'We'll soon find him,' said the sergeant, folding away his notebook and buttoning up his pocket again. 'We'll let you know as soon as we have news.' He led the way out to the car once more, and the constable followed, giving Hanni a warm smile in the guise of reassuring her as he went. They drove silently down the drive, carefully out into the road, and disappeared. Hanni felt better. She returned to the

drawing-room, built the fire up again, and was ready
by the telephone when Stella rang.

'The police thought we should get in touch with
Mr. Graham, Hanni,' she said. She imagined Peter's
reaction if, as had been suggested, the police themselves had told him what had happened. Dreadful as
the duty was, she knew that it was she who must carry
it out. She no longer felt that her anxiety was need-
less; the police clearly thought that Rupert must have
had some sort of accident, though they suggested that
if he had had another fall from the pony he might
be walking home. 'Can you tell me what Mr.
Graham's telephone number is?' she asked.

Hanni searched in the book before her and carefully read out the number of Peter's office. Stella
repeated it after her as she wrote it down.

'Now, I will see to that,' Stella said. 'We must clear
the line, Hanni, in case anyone wants to get through.'
She felt that Rupert, if unharmed but perhaps stranded
somewhere, would surely telephone his own home. He
did not seem the type of thoughtless boy who might
absent himself for hours without letting anyone know
where he was.

'Of course.'

Once again they severed the connection between
them; two women who had never met but who were
now united in a common fear.

II

JOAN sat in the taxi, nursing the poodle puppy. It was coal black, covered in curls, with a minute stick of a tail and very bright eyes. An icy nose touched her hand, and occasionally a tiny pink tongue appeared, questingly, and licked her finger. She could feel the little heart beating fast as the puppy peered about, alertly, wondering where he was going.

The house where Pogo (as he had already been christened) had spent his life so far, with his brothers, sisters, cousins, aunts and other relations, was a sad-looking semi-detached villa in a suburb of north London. Joan had travelled there frugally by tube and bus; but if she were to be back in time for Caroline's wedding, the only hope was to return direct by taxi. If the streets were clear she might just manage it. She relaxed slightly, and Pogo slipped off her knee on to the leather seat of the cab. He scrabbled frantically, and she gently restored him to the warmth of her lap. What a change was in store for him, she thought: Merelands, where she had never been but where, correctly, she imagined soft, deep carpets, polished floors and bowls of flowers, very different from the worn mosaic patterned lino and faint smell of boiled cabbage that characterised his birthplace. She had stood, beside three empty milk bottles, on the tiled step in the shelter of the porch, and rung the bell. The front door was patched with panes of coloured glass. Footsteps, echoing from far beyond the hall, heralded the approach of Mrs. Bridlington, and Joan saw through the orange and purple glass a round figure who was revealed, when she opened the door, as closely resembling a rather plump poodle herself. A mop of mahogany curls fringed her face and beady brown eyes inspected the caller.

'Miss Bentham? Come in.'

Joan obeyed, and was led through the narrow hall to a room at the back of the house where in large boxes various poodle families lay, warmly snuggling, the mothers and their young. The vegetable odour she had already noticed blended here with a damp, woolly, milky smell, and as they entered a shrill yapping from the mothers began, with a descant of shrill squeaks from the pups. Two of the bitches hopped out of their nests and stood with tails at right angles to their bodies, legs stiffly planted, loudly protesting.

Shrieking above the din, Mrs. Bridlington pointed out the charms of the various candidates for Joan's selection. Pogo and a tiny white cousin had the most expressive faces of them all, and Joan chose the black one because she doubted her ability to keep the other looking clean enough through the rest of the day so that he would make a suitably dazzling first appearance.

He shivered and squirmed. Joan felt sorry for him, plucked from his family circle and now embarking on a long, lonely journey. She wondered how Peter would cope with him on the train and whether she should get a basket in which he could be carried. It seemed heartless to shut him up, when he was small enough to slip inside a pocket.

The taxi dropped her at the church, which loomed grey and gaunt in the rain. She paid the driver and went quickly up the steps. As she entered and slipped into a pew near the door, still clasping the puppy, another taxi bringing Peter and Caroline drew up outside.

The church was deserted except for the figures of two young men standing before the chancel, and three or four other people sitting in the front pews, but the organ was being played and when Peter and Caroline came into the building it increased its volume as the Trumpet Voluntary rang out. Joan had dreaded the idea of a cold, impersonal service, but now she found that her apprehension had been unfounded. Nicholas had not allowed his bride to dispense with all tradition. There were great urns of spring flowers, tulips, daffodils, irises and lilac, before the altar and at each side of the chancel steps. A small choir of sleek-haired boys sang an anthem and the two short hymns; with their voices, sweet and clear, in the background, Joan was moved by the extreme youth and vulnerability of Caroline as she stood, tall yet so

slight, between the stocky figure of her father and the
lean, angular form of Nicholas. Three heads, one
sandy and slightly bald, one blonde and crowned with
a tiny flower-petalled hat, one dark and shining, were
presented to her gaze. His part in the service over,
Peter stepped back and into one of the pews at the
front of the church. He did not glance in Joan's direction; she did not know whether he knew she was there
until afterwards, when they straggled out of the
church behind the couple. Peter had arranged for
sandwiches and champagne in a private room of a
hotel where he sometimes entertained. Taxis were
waiting to take them there, and Joan found herself
in one with Peter and two men from the studios who
had been in the church. Peter sat beside her, solid in
his black coat, with his hat on his knee, while the
others perched opposite on the folding seats alternately
exclaiming at the slyness of Nicholas and Caroline and
admiring the puppy's charms.

The hotel had done wonders at short notice; the
room was brightly lit and gay with flowers, and they
had produced a wedding cake. Soon, the young people
grew gay. Peter had persuaded Caroline to telephone
her flat-mates, Daphne and Jane, and ask them to the
wedding. Neither was able to get to the service, but
each managed to obtain leave for an hour to come
and drink a toast afterwards. Neither showed any
sense of grievance at Caroline's treatment of them;
they ate heartily, drank several glasses of champagne,

promised to have a fine present waiting when the pair returned from their honeymoon and were resigned at the prospect of having someone new in Caroline's place at the flat. Daphne found Felix, one of Nicholas' television friends, good-natured and placid, to talk to; Jane sternly lectured the others until one of them, interrupting, made her suddenly laugh and lose her intensity. They all decided that as they had been done out of a proper wedding with its attendant excitement they would meet again in the evening and continue the celebration when time was less limited. Jane took off her glasses and put them away; Daphne forgot that her heart was broken, grew pink and began to giggle.

Slowly, Peter and Joan drew away from them. A waiter had produced a large box and a saucer of milk for the puppy who now slept, warm and replete, curled in an old blanket, while Joan described his purchase. A burst of laughter came from the little group clustered round Nicholas and Caroline. Suddenly the words and the courage came to Joan.

'I'm going away, Peter,' she said.

He stared at her, not certain at first of her meaning.

'I'm going,' she said again. 'I'm going to America.' And then, when he seemed about to protest, 'Don't say anything. It's for the best. You know it is. You've hated having a bad conscience, you aren't the sort for this kind of thing. Jill Taylor is quite competent to take over my work, and I'll find a new junior before I leave.'

'But Joan—' he put his hand on her arm.

'No, say nothing,' she told him again, moving quickly away because if he touched her she must weaken. Her eyes were very bright. 'We needn't say any more. I'm going to talk to Caroline now.'

She walked away across the room; he saw that she held herself unusually erect. Caroline's happy face smiled even more warmly as they began to talk, and he realised for the first time that she had a real affection for Joan. He felt an intense sadness: Joan had meant what she said, and he knew he would have to accept it. He saw years of loneliness stretching ahead while he pandered to Meriel and longed for the courage to end the pretence. He knew he would never openly rebel; too many years of habit tied them, too many outward bonds of convention.

Caroline, towing her tall young husband by the sleeve, came over.

'Daddy, cheer up,' she cried. 'It's a wedding, not a wake. You do look glum.'

'Sir, I know I should have come to see you,' Nicholas began anxiously.

With an effort, Peter laughed. 'Don't worry, my boy,' he said, and felt very old. 'We'll talk when you come back from Italy. There will be lots of time then, and you'll have found out what an extravagance you've acquired.'

'Daddy!' Caroline protested. 'Nick, don't you believe him. I'm frightfully thrifty really and I can cook quite well, you know that.'

'Well, I can, anyway, so I'll soon teach you,' said Nicholas with a grin. Peter looked at this stranger to whom his beloved daughter had so suddenly pledged her life. What would happen to them both? Was there more between them than he and Meriel had ever had? Would they make a success of their life together? It was impossible to foretell, but watching them, trying to see beneath the surface banter of their conversation, Peter felt that there was hope: perhaps because Caroline had been shrewd enough to understand her own mother she would be warned, and perhaps Nicholas had the perception to realise his own unique good fortune.

'We'll take the poodle,' Caroline was saying now, on her knees by the box and crooning over Pogo. 'Isn't he sweet? I do think Joan's clever to have found him. We've decided to go to Timpsley on the way to the boat and get it over. The puppy will help, and it'll be miles better for him than going in the train.'

'Well, that's true enough,' said Peter. He had not been looking forward to his journey with Pogo. He looked at Nicholas enquiringly.

'Of course we'll take him,' said Nicholas. 'I feel badly enough about Mrs. Graham as it is.'

'Never mind. She'll get used to the idea in time,'

said Peter in a hard voice. 'Right, my dear,' he went on to Caroline. 'You take him. And good luck.'

'We're going now, Daddy dear,' said Caroline, and she kissed him. Peter swallowed. He had seldom felt so moved. He hugged her, unable to speak, and then shook hands with Nicholas.

'I'll take great care of her, sir,' said Nicholas steadily.

Peter cleared his throat.

'Bless you both,' he said gruffly, and clapped the young man heartily on the shoulder.

'Give me the puppy, Joan,' said Caroline, wrapping her coat across her body and standing very tall.

Joan bent and gently withdrew Pogo from his cosy bed. She handed him to Caroline, who slid the writhing little bundle into the crook of one arm. She glanced from her father to Joan, seemed about to speak and then changed her mind. She kissed Joan, seized Nicholas' hand, and was gone.

Peter and Joan travelled back to the office together. For the first few minutes they did not speak at all; then they began to exchange stilted commonplace remarks about the wedding. As Joan repeated something she had heard Nicholas say and which showed, she thought, his sterling worth, Peter interrupted.

'Joan, you said you were finished with me,' he said.

'That wasn't quite how I put it, Peter,' she replied. Her voice was low but calm. 'You'll see, when you've had time to get used to the idea, you'll be relieved.

You've had nothing from me that's really made any of this worth while for you. It's not too late for you to patch things up at home; you must still care for her or you wouldn't worry so much about her birthday.'

Peter stared out of the window at the passing scene. Traffic, impatient or resigned, surged by; people beneath umbrellas hurried along, jostled on the pavements. He spoke dully.

'Meriel only minds about what shows,' he said. 'She likes to observe convention.'

'There must have once been more,' Joan insisted. 'When you were young.'

Peter shook his head.

'Perhaps,' he said. 'We had youth, of course. One mistakes that for all sorts of things.' He sighed. 'You haven't stolen anything she valued, Joan.'

Joan was sitting, tense, balanced forward on her seat. She gripped her handbag tightly. Lurching as the cab swirled round a corner, she reached out quickly for the strap at the side of it to prevent herself from being flung against him by the momentum.

'I've had a lot of your time and attention, Peter,' she said. 'I don't regret any of it, I've been very happy. But I've no right to it.'

He said, slowly, 'What will you do?'

She saw that she had convinced him. Perhaps, at bottom, she had hoped he would prevail and persuade her; as the raw ache that would take so many months to heal opened inside her, she said brightly, 'Oh, I'll be all right. I told you, I'm going to America. I've always wanted to do that, and I must hurry before I get too old. I know you'll give me a marvellous reference, and I'll be able to work my way across the States. I'll manage very well.'

'I know it's all been very unfair,' Peter said.

'It isn't that. Please don't think that's what I feel,' Joan said. Now, when the battle was over and there was only the final skirmish and the clearing up to do, it was safe to touch him, and she put her hand on his arm. 'I'll never forget anything, and I'll always be grateful, Peter.'

Absently he took her hand in his, still looking miserably out of the window, and patted it. She pressed her lips together. He had not protested, never tried to make her change her mind; it had been an unopposed victory.

'Here we are,' she said brightly, thankful to see the familiar office building looming up as the taxi slowed. She leaned forward, withdrawing her hand from his and reached for the door-handle. He stretched past her and opened it, and she got out. She left him standing in the rain, paying off the driver, while she ran inside and rushed blindly upstairs, forcing back the tears that burnt against her eyelids. She would not cry; there would be time for weeping later.

She heard Peter's footsteps, slow and heavy, coming past her door; they paused outside, then carried on, as he walked by, down the corridor, to his office.

12

AFTER the police car had left, Stella went back into the small, rather untidy sitting-room. She made herself comfortable in her favourite chair, with her feet up on a battered leather pouffe and a cushion in the small of her back, and picked up the baby's jacket that she was knitting; but it was no good, she could not settle. The image of Rupert's sensitive, thin-featured face haunted her mind; she pictured him lying unconscious somewhere on the common, perhaps kicked by the pony but anyway drenched with the rain that was still falling. If only she could help to find him! And if only she had insisted that he did not ride the pony home! He must have been more shaken than he appeared, perhaps suffering from delayed concussion; the pony might have misbehaved again and Rupert been unable to control him. How would she face Peter when he came home? She had telephoned his office, but discovered that both he and his personal secretary were out, and not expected back till after four o'clock. She had not liked to leave a message that might be misconstrued, so she had rung up her own husband, told him the story, and they had agreed that she should get in touch with Peter later. By then possibly there would be news of the boy. The police would make enquiries from all the hospitals, and they would search the district. If there was no trace of Rupert as dusk approached she thought they would enlist the aid of the Army so that cordons of men could hunt for him. The pony would be traced; someone would see that grey, mudstained, riderless creature and take action. If only she could, herself, go out on foot and look for him, instead of sitting idly by waiting till it was time to telephone to his father. But what use would she be, up on the common in the wet, a heavily-burdened, slow-moving pregnant woman? She sighed, and tried once more to concentrate on her knitting, but it was impossible. She abandoned the idea, thrusting the wool and needles back into their polythene bag, and hoisted herself clumsily to her feet. She went out to the kitchen, where she had left her soaking mackintosh spread out near the boiler to dry, and put it on, tied a woollen scarf over her head, slipped into her rubber ankle boots, and went out into the rain. She would go up to Merelands and wait with Hanni; Peter could be telephoned just as easily from there, and if Rupert returned hurt the Swiss girl might need her aid.

She walked up the hill as quickly as her bulk would allow, trudging to the main road where she would soon be able to catch a bus. They passed frequently up there, but only every hour along the lane through

Timpsley Green. There was a wooden shelter at the stop, and she waited there, sitting screened from the rain on the bench inside. After a few minutes a bus arrived, and before long she was turning in to the gate of Merelands. She and Hugh had often passed the house and tried to picture the life that went on within. They met Peter and Meriel occasionally at local parties, but few of their friends were mutual and Stella had never exchanged more than a few words with Meriel. She had gleaned an impression of costly complacence, and had not enjoyed the condescension she felt in the other's manner while they were forced to speak. She had a theory that most adults suffered from one or another feeling of inadequacy, and tried to believe that Meriel concealed shyness behind her veneer of superiority; but she remained convinced that Meriel, if not wholly censorious, at least despised her thoroughly. This did not worry Stella; she was absorbed in her own life, her mature, miraculously found happiness with Hugh, but she liked Peter and thought he deserved more from life than what she felt Meriel would give.

When she rang the front-door bell at Merelands, Hanni came running through the house to open it. She looked in astonishment at Stella, who realised too late that she should have telephoned the girl and warned her she was coming. She explained quickly who she was and why she had come. Hanni, after one swiftly-concealed glance at her shape, led her indoors, and said that there was still no news of Rupert.

Stella was soon sitting very comfortably in Meriel's drawing-room, resting by the blazing fire while Hanni made some tea. She began to think she had acted in foolish haste by coming, until she realised that the girl was glad to have the little task of looking after her to keep her occupied. She saw all Meriel's birthday cards arranged among the china ornaments and Dresden figures on the mantelpiece and wondered idly how many years they celebrated. She supposed that she and Meriel must both be much of an age, yet here was she, belatedly pregnant once again when a more seemly occupation might be catching up on culture, or good works. She thought of the two sons of her earlier, ill-fated marriage, nineteen and twenty-one now, both at red-brick universities and keeping themselves through this vacation with temporary work. They did not condemn her or Hugh; they were glad of her present contentment. She laid her hand upon her stomach, as if to reassure the new life within that it too would have its share of love, and hoped her hurried journey up to Merelands had not harmed it. She felt heavy, and tired of her enormous size, but strong.

Hanni came in, carrying a tray beautifully laid with the best china and a silver tea-pot. Stella basked briefly in the luxury of these refinements and of being waited on. As Hanni seemed about to leave her, she said, 'Aren't you going to have a cup too, Hanni? I'm sure you need one.' She smiled at the plump, pretty girl who could not be much older than her Robin.

'I have mine in the kitchen, yes?' Hanni said. She hovered doubtfully.

'Why not bring your cup in here?' Stella suggested, and while the girl was fetching it she wondered if she had undermined the domestic structure of Meriel's establishment. If it were not for the anxiety about Rupert which had brought her here, she would have looked forward with amusement to the possibility of Meriel returning to discover Hanni entertaining her to tea.

At four-fifteen, when once again she telephoned to Peter, he was in conference with a client and could not be interrupted, but Stella was able to speak to his secretary. She could hear the alarm which her news brought to the low, rather even-pitched voice.

'Oh, how awful! I'll tell him at once, of course. I expect he'll catch the next train down,' said Joan. 'I'll ring you back.' She sounded capable; Stella pictured a plump woman in her forties, with spectacles, in a hound's-tooth checked skirt and hand-knitted jumper of elaborate pattern. Her efficiency did not mask her concern.

'Tell him the police are searching,' Stella said. 'Try to reassure him.'

'I'll do my best.'

Stella did not envy her the task; she felt she had been let off lightly by not speaking direct to Peter.

Slowly she replaced the receiver. The telephone in Meriel's drawing-room was an apple-green instrument, toning well with the furnishings. Stella returned to the sofa and sat down again. Hanni had removed the tea tray and was in the kitchen washing up. It was warm and very comfortable in the quiet room; Stella sank back against the soft cushions and closed her eyes.

When she opened them at a sudden sound, it was to find a policeman, cap under arm, standing over her clearing his throat. He allowed her a few seconds in which to gather her wits, and then spoke.

'We've found the young gentleman, madam. He's been taken to Bearton Cottage Hospital. As we haven't yet found his mother I wondered if you'd mind coming down there with me. You're a friend of the family, I understand.'

'Er—yes—yes I am.' Stella supposed that she was, of the male half of it. She got up at once. 'Of course I'll come. Is he badly hurt?'

'No, we don't think so,' said the sergeant. 'We found him wandering about on the common, he didn't seem very sure of where he was. So far there's no sign of the pony.'

Stella hoped a passing gypsy had appropriated Martian and his tack.

'We'd better let his father know,' she said. 'May I ring him first? Perhaps the maid would pack his pyjamas and toothbrush while I do that, he'll need them, won't he?'

'Very probably,' said the sergeant. 'I'll just go and ask her.' He went out, to interrupt Hanni and the constable who were sitting in the kitchen getting acquainted.

Stella crossed to the telephone once again, and soon she was speaking to Peter. He told her that he was on the point of leaving; a train was due to depart in fifteen minutes and if he were lucky he would catch it. She resisted the urge to embark upon self-recrimination, and simply gave him the bare facts as she knew them, reiterating that the sergeant was certain Rupert was not badly hurt, particularly as he had been walking when found. He said that he would go straight to the Bearton Cottage Hospital, and Stella promised to wait there with Rupert, or near if she were not allowed to see him, till he came. There was no time to let Hugh know what had happened: the sergeant stood waiting by the door with Rupert's suitcase already in the car.

'I'm ready now,' Stella said, and went with him.

13

AFTER Stella had left in the police car, Hanni experienced a great feeling of anti-climax. Rupert was safe; that was the important thing, and though it seemed as if he must be hurt, no one thought he was in any danger. She tidied up the drawing-room, shaking the cushions and putting more logs on the fire; then she went back to the kitchen and made herself a cup of very strong coffee. There seemed to be nothing she could do that would be useful; how long, she wondered, before Meriel returned? The constable had said that the police were looking for her and would probably soon find her at her meeting and tell her what had happened. Hanni felt sure that Rupert's parents would not now go out to dinner, so she laid the dining-room table. There were plenty of eggs; she could make omelettes, or a fricassee from the remains of the chicken. This thought reminded her that Rupert's plate was still in the oven. She took it out, scraped the dried-up food into the boiler, and washed it, rubbing hard with Brillo to get the singed fragments off. She had just put it away when she heard the tyres of a car in the drive. It must be Meriel, returned.

Hanni hurried to meet her, with sentences of explanation forming in her mind, ready to be uttered instantly.

But it was not the Humber. A cream-coloured sports car, with its hood up against the weather, had stopped close to the front door, and from it was getting a very tall young man whom Hanni had never seen before. He went round to the passenger's door, and Hanni saw that it was Caroline whom, with immense care, he was helping to emerge. She clung to him, laughing up at him, at the same time clasping some small object to her. The sentimental Hanni recognised at once that here was an *affaire de cœur*, and her spirits began to rise.

'Mam'selle Caroline, it is you!' she exclaimed, smiling.

'Hullo, Hanni.' Still laughing, Caroline drew the young man with her into the house.

'Oh, but I am glad to see you!' Hanni cried, standing back from the doorway to let them pass. 'Come in, come in. The drawing-room fire is brightly burning. Please enter and grow warm. Oh, and what is this you have? How adorable!' She had seen the puppy. Pogo gazed up at the round beaming face that bent over him and licked his whiskers.

'It's for Mother. It's her birthday present from Father. He didn't bring it yesterday because he couldn't have hidden it, he thought,' Caroline said. 'Where is she?'

Hanni stopped and put her hands on her hips.

'Miss, your mother, she is not here. From home she is.' Idiom deserted Hanni under stress.

'Oh.' Caroline looked put out. 'Well, where is she? She won't be long, I suppose?'

'She is at the Drama with Mrs. Manners,' said Hanni.

Caroline looked puzzled, and then she realised what the Swiss girl meant.

'Mother does amateur dramatics,' she explained to Nicholas, who had listened in patient silence to this exchange.

'Ah, but how good that you are come, Miss Caroline,' Hanni was continuing. 'Now you shall be here to break the news when Mrs. Graham returns.'

'News? But that's why we're here.' Caroline now looked bewildered. 'Oh, you can't mean about us.' She frowned. 'You don't know.'

'It is about Rupert that I speak,' said Hanni severely. First things first: romance was important, but it did not merit attention ahead of Rupert's plight.

'Rupert? Why, what's the matter?' At last Caroline realised that something was wrong. Nicholas, already uneasy because he feared an embarrassing scene with Meriel lay ahead, put his arm round her shoulders.

'He was lost,' Hanni told them. 'He went riding and did not return, but now he is found, and lies hurt at the hospital.'

'Oh, Hanni!' Caroline gasped, and then, 'that beastly pony, he was always too much for Rupert. I kept meaning to have it out with Mother about it. Is he bad, Hanni?'

'All is not yet known,' Hanni declared. 'The policeman said he thought it was not serious.'

'The policeman?' Caroline repeated, incredulous.

'Yes. Your mother was not here, but Mrs. Wheeler came.'

It took Nicholas, intervening with calm authority, some minutes to get a clear account from Hanni of the day's events. When at last her recital ended he gave Caroline a little hug.

'Don't worry, darling,' he urged. 'He's probably just knocked himself out. Kids are tough.'

'Rupert isn't. You don't know him,' Caroline said. 'He hated that pony. I kept meaning to do something about it, but now it's too late. Mother made him ride. He was scared stiff. I used to think he'd get over it, but Martian's a brute, he needs someone much stronger to handle him. Oh, poor Rupert.'

'Darling, he's probably not bad,' Nicholas said again. 'We'll know soon, this Mrs. Wheeler will be sure to telephone. If not, we'll ring the hospital. How far is Bearton?'

'About ten miles,' said Caroline.

Nicholas looked at his watch. 'Well, if they'd only left just before we got here—Mrs. Wheeler and the police, I mean, as Hanni said, they'll only just about be arriving at the hospital now. Let's give them a few minutes to find out the position, and then if she hasn't rung, we'll get through to them.'

'Sir is right, Miss Caroline,' said Hanni, greatly approving of the manner in which Nicholas had taken charge.

'Oh, Hanni, yes, I know he is,' said Caroline. She gave a rather despairing laugh and said, 'you'd better know that "sir" here is my husband. We were married this afternoon.' At this she drew herself up proudly, and watched Hanni's face as it revealed first incredulity and then delight.

'Oh, Miss—Madame, I mean, and Sir, that is good!' she exclaimed.

'Yes, it is,' said Nicholas with a smile. 'We came to tell Mrs. Graham, but now there's this other news about Rupert—' His voice trailed off, for they had all heard a door slam.

'It is Madame your mother,' Hanni said gravely to Caroline. 'You have a surprise for her: I too. You cannot tell both. I first will tell of Rupert.' She walked firmly away before they could prevent her.

'What a splendid girl,' cried Nicholas.

'She is a dear, a real treasure, I can't think why she stays unless it's for love of Rupert,' Caroline said. 'She adores him. Ssh, listen!'

They could hear the sound of voices in the hall; Meriel's predominated, getting louder as she came nearer to the drawing-room where the others waited.

Then they heard Hanni determinedly break in and interrupt.

'Madame, please! The car outside, it is Miss Caroline who has come with a small dog for your birthday and also here is her husband.'

Nicholas slipped his arm down from Caroline's shoulder and took her hand. They stood close together, the puppy, as if aware of impending disaster, trembling as she held it with her other hand.

'Her—what did you say?' they heard.

'His name I do not know,' Hanni said. 'Her husband he is.' Her voice was calm. Only Nicholas recognised the fury underneath.

There was a moment's silence. Caroline imagined her mother pausing outside the door to draw breath and summon her reserves for battle, before she came into the room. Nicholas whispered, with more confidence than he felt, 'Don't worry, darling, it'll be all right,' and kissed her ear. Then the door was flung open and Meriel stood upon the threshold glaring at them both, for once deprived of words.

Caroline seized the chance to speak first and stepped forward. 'Mother, Hanni can't have told you, Rupert's been hurt, he's in Bearton Hospital. He had a riding accident, we don't know yet what happened.'

Meriel stepped into the room and closed the door behind her, shutting out Hanni, who looked aghast. She faced them both, her colour high, and Nicholas, older, more perceptive than his wife, felt a transient pity as she stood, briefly, but only for an instant, at a loss.

'Hanni said—' she began.

Nicholas took Caroline's hand again.

'We were married this afternoon, Mrs. Graham,' he said quietly.

'But—'

Caroline had never before seen her mother irresolute.

'We didn't want any fuss, Mother,' she said. 'I'm of age. This is Nicholas Fraser, my husband.' She turned to Nicholas and smiled at him with pride. When she saw the joy in their two young faces, Meriel was pierced by an emotion that she did not try to identify, and would not have acknowledged, anyway, as envy. 'And this,' Caroline went on, holding out the puppy, 'is Daddy's present. Happy birthday, Mother.' Too late, she realised that this was not a tactful greeting under the circumstances. 'Our present's in the car,' she rushed on. 'We'll get it later.'

Meriel glanced down at the puppy.

'Oh—yes, how sweet,' she said vaguely, and then she understood what this meant. 'You've seen your father. He knows,' she pounced.

'Daddy came to our wedding,' Caroline said. 'But he knew nothing about it till today. We didn't tell anyone.' She paused, and then hurried on before Meriel had replied. 'Do you realise that Rupert's hurt? He's in hospital.'

Nicholas released Caroline's hand.

'This must all be a dreadul shock, Mrs. Graham,' he said. 'Won't you sit down?' He moved the chair nearest to Meriel a little closer to her, hoping she would subside into it, but she ignored him. Speaking directly to Caroline she spoke in a low voice.

'How could you do this to me?' she said.

'Mother, we'll talk about all that later. Don't you understand, Rupert's hurt, he may be dying!' Her voice broke, and Nicholas hurried back to her.

'Darling, no, the police said it wasn't bad,' he said. 'Mrs. Graham, may I drive you down to the hospital?'

But Meriel would not listen. Her face had become very flushed. Anxiously he wondered if she might have a stroke, and thought that the marriage could hardly have begun in a worse atmosphere.

'I'll never forgive you, Caroline,' her mother said. 'Nor your father. Nor you,' turning at last to Nicholas.

'Mother!' Caroline was tense. 'How do I get through to you? Don't you ever think of anyone else but yourself? Can't you realise that Rupert may need you?'

Nicholas, new to this situation, thought she was harsh and that her mother had been stunned by the double blow. He shook his head slightly at her, but Caroline did not see. She stared fiercely at her mother.

'Please let me take you to the hospital,' Nicholas pleaded, but his words were ignored.

'You're pregnant,' Meriel said at last. 'That's the

explanation. It must be. You little tramp. And as for you—' she added to Nicholas, who had gone white.

'That is not true, Mrs. Graham,' he said icily, and Caroline could only wonder at his restraint. Now his earlier tolerance vanished; he saw that Caroline's assessment of her mother was accurate after all, and the guilt he felt about the manner of their marriage disappeared.

'Mother, how could you!' Caroline stood taut, her weight on her toes, looking at her mother as if she were something that had crawled out from under a stone; and so indeed, to the rigid idealism of the girl's youth, she seemed. 'I pity you,' Caroline went on. 'I pity you, oh, I do. I forgive you for what you've just said, because I know you don't understand what it means to love anybody. You just need a—a band of satellites to orbit round you, not a family of human beings. Poor Daddy, poor old Daddy. None of us matters to you except as symbols. A proper mother would be frantic with worry about Rupert, but not you! Oh, no! You're too busy insulting us. Well, I'm all right, I've got Nick, I've escaped, and Rupert will eventually, if he gets better—or even if he doesn't. But there's no escape for Daddy. He'll never leave you. I would, if I were him. He ought to go to Joan, and I've a good mind to tell him so.'

'Joan? What on earth do you mean?' Meriel put a hand to her head. Caroline had never openly rebelled before; now that the moment had come her wrath was all the greater.

'Joan Bentham, of course. You're so wrapped up in your own importance that I don't suppose it's ever occurred to you that Daddy might find love with someone else.'

'Caro—don't—' Nicholas was appalled, and once again he tried to check Caroline, but she would not be stopped.

'Oh, you're safe enough.' Her voice was jeering now, ugly with the rage that consumed her. 'No one knows but me, and I'm glad, glad, glad, to think he's had at least a little happiness. But they'll never have the courage to break away, I know they won't.' She paused, her throat choking with tears, and as Nicholas tried to soothe her she went on, 'don't stop me, Nick. You don't know what Daddy's life is like. I'm not going to say any more. If you won't go to Rupert, Mother, I will. He must have someone of his own. Mrs. Wheeler's gone, but she's not his family. Nick, take me to Rupert.'

'Stella Wheeler?' Meriel, drowning in a nightmare, repeated the name, and then the other one, 'Joan Bentham?' wonderingly.

'And take your dog. Here he is, your birthday present. Perhaps he'll work a miracle,' Caroline cried, thrusting Pogo, who had been terrified by the loud voices coming across his head, into Meriel's reluctant arms. 'Come on, Nick.' She stalked out of the room, followed by Nicholas who felt extremely distressed.

Left alone, Meriel stood staring blankly at the wall before her, holding the tiny, squirming, and now squealing puppy in her hands.

'Joan Bentham,' she said aloud. 'That—that frump. I won't believe it.'

When the telephone began to ring some time later she was still standing there, holding the frightened puppy and staring at the wall.

14

ONCE again Peter was in a taxi driving through the streets of London. He had told the driver to hurry, and now sat forward on the edge of his seat, as though by doing so he might compel the cab to travel faster. The thought that obsessed him, to the exclusion almost of any other, was that he should have understood that Martian's behaviour was not just high spirits but real malice. He ought to have given the matter thought, overruled Meriel for once, and let Rupert escape; or at least he should have taken steps to find a more docile pony.

Joan was right in what she implied : his family had suffered because of his preoccupation with her. Here was Caroline, married all in a moment to a young man of whom he had never heard until today. If he had been a proper, dutiful father such a thing could not have happened, for he would have been in her confidence, or so he told himself, intent upon self-castigation and forgetting that the young have many secrets. He knew Caroline's strictures concerning her mother were accurate; but if he had played his part at home fully, things might not have degenerated so far.

He should have asserted himself, laughed Meriel out of her snobbery and somehow eased the children's paths. As a girl it was her gaiety and self-confidence that had first attracted him; now the one had swamped the other. Her poise had battened on his own humility; ruthlessly she fought to increase her own importance while he and the children struggled in their role of hostages to her whims. It was his own fault; after the war he had immersed himself in his career, intent upon building it up so that he could provide the background Meriel desired, at the same time burying his disillusion in his work. Probably, he thought now, it was this absorption of his that had made her fight so hard for increasing social success, the one acting as a spur upon the other. Then, when despair was slowly rising in him, he had turned to Joan, so that for years he had drifted, a complaisant lodger in his own house.

But it would be different now. Rupert could be rescued, even if it were too late to resurrect any feeling between himself and Meriel.

The taxi jerked to a standstill: they were at Victoria. Peter jumped out, thrusting a handful of coins at the driver, and hurried off through the jostling throng of people travelling and meeting trains. Joan, efficient as ever and calm in any crisis, had looked up the train, for he seldom left as early as this, but even she could not foretell from which platform it would leave, and when at last he got to it the doors were already slamming. He found a seat without trouble, for he was well ahead of the main commuting rush, but he had not had time to buy a paper, nor had he brought anything from the office to keep him busy on the journey. He had left a mass of work for Joan to disentangle. In any case, he could not have concentrated on any reading. Images of Rupert and Caroline in the earlier years sprang to his imagination's eye : the boy, small, defenceless, at the start of his first term away at school, swamped in an overcoat several sizes too big, and staring at his parents when they were about to leave with eyes grown very large.

'What shall I do now?' he had asked, the first words he had spoken since leaving home. He had been borne away by a kindly master to help the Matron sort out jam.

Caroline, Peter saw, aged twelve, all legs and arms and very thin, rushing off to spend every spare second down the road with her bosom friend, Elizabeth. Too late to mend the situation, Peter recognised that it was always Caroline who went to Elizabeth's house, and seldom Elizabeth to Merelands. Now he knew why. Typically, in his depression, he could not remember the many times when he had lived up to the expectations of his children, although if he had asked them, both would have quickly quoted dozens of examples. Today, utterly dejected, Peter felt that he had always failed.

The journey seemed endless. The train was a slow one, stopping at every station along the line. People kept getting in and out, women with shopping and children going home from school with bursting satchels. Impatiently he endured the restless progress.

Joan had been so good today. Mentally he reviewed all she had managed to do. Just before he left she had even found time, and remembered, to give him the small red leather collar, now inscribed, for Pogo, which she had sent a typist to collect.

'You may as well take it with you,' she'd said in a matter-of-fact voice. 'Rupert will be all right, don't worry. That Mrs. Wheeler sounded very sure it wasn't bad. It was very lucky that she knew about it and was there.'

'Yes.' Peter's grasp of what had happened was still hazy, for Stella had given few details on the telephone. 'Very lucky.' He thought how much alike were Joan and Stella, each with a similar view of what was important. If they were ever to meet he knew they would be friends.

But of course, they would never meet, for Joan was going away. He supposed, with weariness, that if he really loved her he would never let her leave; for him, she had been an escape. For her own sake he must let her get away; she was still young enough to build her life again, and he was not. That was all. It did not cross his mind that acting thus, releasing her after so long, might be a form of love.

The train at last reached Timpsley Village and he

got out before it stopped, almost running down the platform, through the barrier and to his car. His keys were tangled among the loose coins in his pocket and he wasted valuable seconds unlocking the door, but he was soon roaring off up the road with the choke right out and a cloud of exhaust in his wake.

After the first mile he realised that the situation would not be helped if he were caught speeding, nor if he were to have a smash himself; and he slowed up, and drove more reasonably for the rest of the way to Bearton. He knew the hospital, for Hanni had once spent a short time there having her appendix removed. He had driven her in and fetched her home, and visited her three times to Meriel's twice, so that he was familiar with the approach and general lay-out, and knew the porters by sight. The one now on duty plainly remembered him; he said that Rupert was shaken, had a broken arm and might be slightly concussed, but no more.

'The lady's in Matron's office,' went on the porter. 'And the young lady and gentleman as well.'

'What?' But Peter realised that it must be Caroline and Nicholas whom the porter meant. He went along the dark passage, where the walls were painted brown and the lino was spinach-green, and found Matron's office round a distant corner. Inside, Stella was seated in the armchair and Nicholas and Caroline were leaning against the wall, all drinking sherry.

'Good heavens, what are you all up to?' he exclaimed, for they were all giggling in the aftermath of strong emotion. Stella made an effort.

'He's quite all right, Peter. Matron's gone to get him. They say he can go home, they're just seeing to his arm and patching up his cuts.'

'Matron thought we all needed treating for shock,' Caroline said. 'And when she heard about Nick and me she produced sherry instead of hot, sweet tea. Wasn't it sporting of her?'

Nicholas was poking about in Matron's little cupboard.

'I'm afraid there's no whisky, sir,' he said, and before Peter could stop him he poured out a glass of Matron's sherry for his father-in-law.

Peter accepted it without protest, and drank it in a gulp, not caring about Matron's possible reaction to their making free with her hospitality. He listened while the others told him what had happened to Rupert; no one seemed to know quite how he and the pony had finally parted company.

'We'd better let them know at home that we're bringing him back,' he said.

Caroline, calmer now, replied, 'Nick's already done that, Daddy.'

'Oh, good.'

There was no more to be said. Everyone concentrated on their sherry and Peter poured himself a second glass, mentally resolving to send Matron a case of it the next day. Very soon the door opened and Matron came in, leading Rupert by his sound arm. The other was in a sling across his chest.

'Just a greenstick, lucky boy, he's been spared a plaster,' said Matron cheerfully. She was a round little woman with bright eyes and red cheeks, reminding Peter of a robin. 'Good evening, Mr. Graham. I remember you; your Swiss help came to us for her appendectomy, if I am not mistaken.'

'Yes, indeed,' said Peter, amazed by this feat of memory. He looked, not at Matron, but at his son, and found to his horror that he felt curiously choked. Rupert looked very pale, and there was a strip of sticking plaster over one eye. 'Well, old chap, what have you been up to?' His voice sounded gruff.

Rupert grinned feebly, and Matron answered for him.

'Keep him quiet,' she instructed. 'We're short of beds, or we wouldn't let you take him away, but it won't hurt him to go home. He'll need a few days in bed as he's had a bit of a bang. Your own doctor will see him in the morning.'

Peter felt himself reproved for curiosity. 'Oh, right,' he said. 'We can hear all about what happened later. The main thing is, you're still in one piece, Rupert.'

'Only just,' said Rupert. The pupils of his eyes, dilated with fatigue, shone blackly.

Caroline moved restlessly.

'We'll go now,' she said. 'Come on, Nick.' She kissed her father, then her brother, lightly on the cheek, hesitated before Stella and finally kissed her too. Nicholas, with a shy grin, mumbled 'goodbye' all round, and they departed.

'Who was that with Caro?' Rupert asked.

No one felt equal to explaining now.

'That's Nicholas. A sound chap,' said Peter heartily. 'We'll tell you about him tomorrow. Come along, old man.' Like many men, he was at a loss when faced with physical calamity. It seemed important to appear calm yet brisk. He put his arm lightly round Rupert's shoulder, where his tweed riding jacket was draped over his injured arm.

'The porter has Rupert's mackintosh. I'm afraid it was very torn,' said Matron. 'We'll collect it on our way.' She moved to the door, and then paused to look at Stella. 'Quite sure you don't want to stay with us, Mrs. Wheeler?' she asked.

Stella laughed. 'No, not tonight, Matron,' she said. 'I'm all right. I'll stick to when we've booked me in.'

'Good. Well, it won't be long,' said Matron. 'Ready, everyone?'

The little procession went out, with Matron and Peter supporting Rupert and Stella following behind. The porter came out of his cubicle in the hall with Rupert's mackintosh wrapped in brown paper and bundled it into the boot of Peter's car. They arranged the boy comfortably on the back seat and covered him with blankets which Peter promised to return next day. Stella got into the front seat beside Peter, and turned round, awkwardly because of her bulk, to smile at the patient.

'We'll soon have you tucked up in bed, Rupert,' said Peter. 'But I shan't drive fast because I don't want to jolt you. O.K.?'

'O.K.,' said Rupert.

Peter started the car and they drove slowly away, with Matron and the porter standing framed in the doorway waving them off. No one felt much like talking. Stella was tired and her back ached. She longed to bombard Peter with questions about Caroline and Nicholas, but knew that she must not. Hugh would, in time, be able to tell her all that had happened. She was tempted, too, to explain and condemn her own part in the drama that was, luckily, ending without disaster; she could not forget that she had allowed Rupert to ride away on his pony that morning. But this was not the moment for the self-indulgence of confession and she remained silent.

Rather drowsily, Rupert said, 'You came home early, Dad.'

'Yes.'

'Lucky it was Mother's birthday. I mean, lucky you were coming home early so you could take me back,' Rupert said, trying to be clear.

'Yes, wasn't it?' Peter realised that Rupert had no idea of the anxiety he had caused. Meriel must somehow be prevented from telling him until he was strong enough to enjoy the thought of his own importance.

'Did you get Mother's present?'

Peter, with new perception, understood that the diminutive 'Mum' which Rupert had used so often and which Meriel had disliked, would not be used again. He felt a great sadness.

'Did you, Dad?' The voice held now a touch of impatience, but Peter hardly noticed that in the rush of gratitude that he felt on hearing himself so addressed. He had always believed that the abbreviation was in the nature of an endearment, like a nickname.

'Yes, I did.'

'What is it?'

'A poodle puppy. A black one,' Peter said.

'Oh.' Rupert thought about it. 'Very appropriate,' he said then. 'It's just what was needed. I expect it's rather sweet.'

'Yes, it is quite,' said Peter. 'It's a miniature; very small.' For the first time Peter thought of Pogo as an entity, one who would create his own important position in the life of the household, perhaps deflecting censure from others. He might, in fact, prove to be the best present yet. 'Here we are,' he said.

The lights were on in the house, and the front door opened as they came to a standstill. Hanni came hurrying out. The rain had stopped, and the air was still.

Rupert said suddenly, 'I don't know where Martian is, Dad.'

Peter, on the point of helping him out of the car, paused.

'He vanished,' Rupert said.

'He'll turn up,' Peter prophesied. 'Don't worry. I don't expect he'll come to any harm. You're safe, and that's the main thing.' He began the business of extracting Rupert, who was by now feeling rather wobbly, out of the car. Hanni assisted with a sturdy arm, and no one noticed when it was that Meriel made her appearance on the scene; she was ignored. Stella, fending for herself, went into the drawing-room and sat down until she should be remembered and taken home. It was too early yet for Hugh to be back, otherwise she could have telephoned for him to fetch her; she knew that she was too tired to make her own way home by bus. She settled down, with a cushion in the small of her back, to wait.

Presently Peter appeared.

'Stella, are you all right? I'm so sorry to leave you like this, but I'll run you home as soon as I can. You must be all in. I can't ever thank you for what you've done,' he said. 'Have some sherry? Or would you like anything else?'

She shook her head.

'Don't worry, Peter. I'm very comfortable,' she said. 'You see to Rupert.'

Looking relieved, Peter went away promising not to be long, and once more Stella was left. It was Meriel who came next. She looked paler than Stella remembered, but that was not surprising. Apart from that, she was as poised as ever.

'I must thank you, Mrs. Wheeler,' she said. Stella wanted to giggle : she felt like a kitchenmaid in the unlikely position of being thanked by a duchess, such was Meriel's air of condescension. It was obvious that gratitude did not come easily to her. 'Rupert has caused a lot of trouble.'

'It wasn't his fault,' Stella said. 'I'm glad he's all right.' She thought, what the hell, what do I care about Meriel, and plunged recklessly on : 'You know, Mrs. Graham, that pony's too much for him.'

Meriel set her lips. 'Rupert lacks determination,' she said. 'He could easily manage Martian if he tried harder. But never mind, I mustn't bore you with our domestic problems. Peter will drive you home in a few minutes. I must ask you to excuse me as I have to go and change. We are dining out this evening; it's my birthday, and Peter insists every year on taking me out.' She smiled, as if at a foible. 'Forgive me if I leave you,' she said, and sailed graciously out of the room.

Stella stared after her. Slowly she realised that Meriel believed herself to be speaking the truth, but she was certain that the last thing Peter would want to do, with Rupert in bed upstairs, was to go out. Surely they would cancel their plans? She forced herself to admit that, with the boy no doubt soundly sleeping off the effect of his adventures, Hanni was quite able and competent to be left in attendance, but she could not understand how, after such an experience, Meriel could even wish to go out. Of course, she had been spared the worry and strain which everyone else had endured through the day, for she had been ignorant of Rupert's plight until after he was found. All the same, Stella could not see herself remaining so unmoved. She wondered whether the household would spring any more surprises.

Soon Hanni came into the room. She stood inside the door with her hands demurely folded and said, 'Mr. Graham comes, Madame. He will be only a few minutes. I show you the puppy, yes?' She did not wait for Stella's reply, but went over to a big grocer's cardboard carton, lined with old woollies, which Stella now saw against the wall, and lifted it up. 'Isn't he sweet?' Hanni crooned, carrying it over so that Stella could see Pogo curled up inside, his stomach still distended with the feast of bread and milk on which he had earlier gorged himself.

'He's a pet,' Stella said. 'Rupert will love him.'

Hanni nodded, and they smiled at one another, liking each other.

'I come to see your baby, please?' Hanni asked shyly. 'On my day off? Mr. Graham will perhaps tell me when it has arrived. I help you,' she promised.

'Oh, do Hanni, of course. I'd love you to see her,' said Stella warmly. With two sons already, she longed for a daughter and was convinced that her baby was a girl. She pushed aside the thought of Meriel's displeasure if she learned that Hanni was spending her off-duty time in Timpsley Green helping with the infant Wheeler.

'Good. It is fixed,' said Hanni calmly. 'I go now to prepare soup for Rupert. Then he sleeps. Goodnight, Madame.'

'Goodnight, Hanni.'

Stella watched as the Swiss girl returned Pogo, who had not stirred, to his corner, and then went out. A moment later Peter's heavy tread could be heard on the stairs and he came in, looking tired and rather crumpled. Stella felt suddenly furious; what a beastly, selfish woman, she thought, dragging this poor man out after all he's been through today.

'Peter, you can't go out tonight, you're exhausted,' she said.

'I am,' he agreed. 'And you're right, I'm not going. I did tell Meriel, but she chose not to hear me. She'll find I meant it.' He smiled. 'Stella, could you possibly bear to come up and say goodnight to Rupert. He wants to thank you.'

'Of course I'll come,' she said, and struggled to her feet.

'Thanks.'

Peter led the way, and they went up the shallow, carpeted stairs and along the passage to Rupert's room. Expensive comfort was manifest throughout each step of the way, and Stella could not repress a feeling of envy, but she thought, too, that her own shabby house had a happier relaxed atmosphere.

Rupert was sitting up in bed propped against pillows, with his blue pyjama jacket pinned across his sling.

'Goodnight, Rupert. I hope your arm will soon be better,' said Stella. She knew now that it had already been fractured after his fall in the morning. Matron at the hospital, to whom she had revealed what had happened, had roundly declared her free from blame; the doctor, she said, had been surprised when the X-ray showed the extent of the damage, for he had thought Rupert had merely severely bruised himself; but Stella would never forget.

'Dad's going to get me another pony. A quieter one,' Rupert said. 'It's a pity I couldn't conquer Martian, but I'll improve with practice.'

Stella stared at Peter. She had thought the boy would never want to ride again.

'That's the stuff,' said Peter calmly. 'We'll have you steeplechasing yet.'

Rupert chuckled.

'I rather doubt it, Dad, thanks all the same,' he said, and added to Stella, 'I'll come and see you, like you said I could, Mrs. Wheeler.'

'Yes, please do, Rupert,' said Stella. With Peter dropping in on his way home from the station, Hanni on her day off, and now Rupert when he could, she thought that soon she would see more of the Graham family than Meriel.

'I must take Mrs. Wheeler home now,' said Peter.

'Mr. Wheeler will be wondering where she's got to. I'll pop up and see you when I get back, but I hope you'll be asleep by then. Hanni will be up soon with your supper.'

'I missed lunch,' Rupert realised. A big chunk was missing from the middle of his day, gone for ever from his memory. He remembered riding away up the hill from Stella's house, and striking across the common, filled with a new determination to vanquish Martian; but he had been hampered by the pain in his arm which made it impossible for him to take any strain upon it. The pony, told to trot, had broken into a canter, then put his head down. Hauling on the reins as best he could with his sound arm, Rupert had not been able to make any impression on the animal's iron mouth. Branches had torn at them as they rushed by, and then Martian, swerving to avoid a hole, had dislodged him. Rupert had sailed over the pony's head, but he could not recollect striking the ground. His next memory was of walking along, stumbling through puddles and brambles trying to find the right path, and unable to recognise where he was. Of Martian there was no sign. Suddenly, staggering along, Rupert had met a policeman prowling through the bracken with his truncheon in his hand thrusting aside the bushes.

'Never mind, you can make it up tomorrow,' said Peter. 'You've nothing to do for a few days but lie in bed eating and sleeping.'

'And reading?' Rupert said anxiously.

'I expect so,' said Peter, hoping the doctor would agree when he came in the morning.

'Goodnight, Rupert,' said Stella. She wanted to kiss him, but knew that he was too old, so she patted his sound arm instead.

Peter followed her out of the room and down the stairs. Meriel was nowhere to be seen and the house was silent.

'I'll be with you in a minute, Stella,' said Peter, and disappeared into the kitchen. He came back very quickly and said, 'Well, that's that. Ready?' He looked jaunty, almost defiant. 'Hugh'll be about back now,' he said. 'I'll beg a noggin off him, if you can put up with the Grahams a bit longer.'

Stella remembered that he had told Rupert he would come and see him when he returned from Timpsley Green, but expected to find him asleep by that time. He intended, then, not merely to drop her home but to come in, deliberately. It was a gesture; she knew Meriel had never had a suspicion of his other visits. She felt like cheering aloud.

'If he isn't back, you must wait till he comes,' she said, and laughed.

15

IT was nearly seven o'clock when Joan left the office
that evening. She put the cover over her typewriter
and pushed the chair back under her desk, as she did
every day before leaving. By now everyone else had
left the premises of Graham and Linnit, even Bruce,
Peter's clerk, who often stayed late poring over vast
tomes as he checked references, or reading lengthy
depositions. Joan was never sure whether he stayed
from love of his work, or because he dreaded returning
to his home in Ealing where his wife kept two budge-
rigars, a canary and a cat, and spent her days plan-
ning their welfare to the exclusion of her husband's.
She seldom answered any of his remarks, but frequently conversed for hours, somewhat one-sidedly,
with her pets. Joan had once been invited to tea on a
Sunday; the birds had hopped around the room perch-
ing on chairs or the pelmets, and the cat, curiously
attached to them, had prowled round scratching the
carpet, and Joan's stockings, and had finally sprung
on to her lap, covering her with fine black hairs. Her
hostess had never addressed her directly: all her conversation was aimed at the birds or the cat, even if her

remarks were of the 'somebody might like some more tea' variety. It was disconcerting, when one was aspiring to be a polite guest, to find one's comments answered with chirrups and twitters. After that day, Joan had felt a new warmth towards Bruce and often went out of her way to help him.

He had gone, however, at six this evening; and the junior staff had left right on time, eager to escape: one had a date, one wanted to wash her hair, and the third was busy making a dress. They had disappeared into the Underground, there to be compressed, as every evening, in the suffering mob that awaited transportation. At least, Joan thought, she would, tonight, be spared the worst of the traffic; that was some comfort. She would not have to stand in a patient queue waiting for her bus, watching several pass before there was one with room for herself.

She went into Peter's office and looked round. She had sorted out the pile of work he had left on his desk, dealing with all that she could and leaving the rest in a neat heap for him to tackle in the morning. There was nothing remaining to show that he had left in a hurry. Well, Rupert was safe, anyway, and that pleasant-sounding Mrs. Wheeler seemed to think he was not seriously hurt. Obscurely, Joan resented Mrs. Wheeler, who played, it seemed, a large part in the home life of the Grahams, although until today she had never heard of her. When they were alone, Peter seldom talked about his life at Timpsley, and it was only by casual references and the occasional disclosures of Caroline when they met that Joan had built up any impression of what it was like. She knew that Peter would not telephone to tell her how the boy really was. Joan had a real affection for Rupert; she had met him sometimes when he had been in London : the children had always loved coming to the office on the slightest pretext, unlike their mother who did not enjoy the rather drab surroundings. Joan wondered if Rupert would follow his father into the firm : if he took up the law, it was more likely that he would seek the Bar, she decided; his sense of drama would find more outlet there.

Now, she had no right to wonder how he was : to-morrow she would discover, for Peter would tell her, and for a few more weeks she would know in outline how he fared; she would hear about Caroline's honey-moon, perhaps even be shown postcards from Italy; she would know when Rupert went back to school. Then she would leave, and she would have to try and put them all, every one of them, out of her mind.

It was a hopeless ambition, of course. How could she, after so many years, stop thinking about the Grahams? Joan moved over to Peter's desk; she stood behind his chair and ran her hands over the back of it, caressing it. Now it seemed impossible that she would go away : she would never be able to thrust him out of her memory and go to another country where she would not see his face again. She would no longer see him when he was worried, pale and anxious as he had been tonight; and she would not see him with the tender, gentle expression so familiar in their moments together.

But the decision was made: sentence was pronounced. She knew that if she merely endured each day as it came she would survive. There were other things: there would be a new job, unfamiliar and challenging; one day there might even be another man, someone who in his turn might want her happiness as she had wanted Peter's. To stand here, as she was now, moping over his desk, was a retrogressive step and she must stop it. She went firmly out of the room and put on her coat, tied the scarf over her head and left the building. As she walked down the road to the bus stop she saw that the rain had stopped; though the streets still gleamed with wet, the sky was clear and patched with a few stars. She breathed deeply, exhaling the mixture of office fug and stale tobacco smoke which she had absorbed during the day, and filled her lungs with the fresh, sweet air. Even the petrol fumes seemed to have been banked down by the dampness. She decided to go down to Berkshire at the weekend. It was weeks since she had seen her parents, and now the thought of their peaceful village drew her.

She wondered how the poodle was getting on at Merelands, and whether Meriel appreciated him. If she were honest, she supposed she would admit to bitter jealousy of Peter's wife, but she did not envy her life in Timpsley, which seemed to be made up of an artificial social progress. Of course, it could not always have been like this; years ago, when there was less money and they were younger, there must have been more to her life with Peter. And how much of the blame for today's situation rested with him? He had neglected his wife, that could not be denied; and he had deceived her. Joan had often wondered how Meriel would react if she were to discover, and now her imagination played briefly with the impossible idea of confronting her. But she knew it could not happen : Meriel's security must never be jeopardised. Perhaps the world needed people like her, insensitive souls who bulldozed their way through life disguised as advertisements for the sanctity of the home.

The bus came. Joan climbed up on to the top deck and was borne along through the city. The lights of London shone on either side of her, and the people of London, made up from so many different nationalities, went about upon their own affairs. Many must have hearts quite as heavy as hers, Joan knew; some must, in fact, be experiencing grief of an even greater and more final sort, facing bereavement, illness, even homelessness. She tried to comfort herself by thinking of the very ordinary, often-met nature of her suffering.

She got off the bus at the stop at the end of her road, and then she did something that was quite unprecedented : she went into the pub on the corner and bought herself a double whisky. It was done on the spur of the moment, because she wanted to put off the moment of going back, alone, into her flat, shutting herself away from the mass of humanity about her.

There were a lot of people in the lounge bar, and she carried her drink away from the counter to a corner. She felt only slightly self-conscious : she had never before gone into a pub by herself, though she would cheerfully have done so with a girl friend : now she did not care who saw her or what they thought. The whisky warmed her; she took the scarf off her head and shook her hair. There were one or two glances in her direction, but she gave an impression of composure which did not invite attention. She was just another dowdy, rather tired, not very young woman calling in for a nip before she went home. She left quite soon, revived by the drink to a state of false cheer, and reflecting that if she were a man this was the sort of moment when she would get drunk. If she were another sort of woman, too, she would have a host of men friends from among whose ranks she would at once whistle one up to take the place of Peter; such a woman would not have sat alone in the pub, unremarked.

But it was more comfortable to be herself : she need think of nothing now but her own misery. She let herself into the flat. There were no letters waiting on the mat; she rarely received any mail by the second post but she still pretended that some wonderful communication from a long-forgotten acquaintance would one day come with news that would alter her whole life.

She kicked off her shoes, leaving them where they lay in the hall, and let her coat slide on to a chair. She had had no lunch, and had little appetite at the wedding; now the whisky, on an empty stomach, was having its effect. She could make no effort to be tidy.

'Just as well, pernickety old maid that I am,' she said aloud, going into the sitting-room. She switched on the fire and sat down on the carpet in front of it, staring at the slowly reddening bar, not thinking of anything. Then, sighing, she heaved herself up again. She must think about food, she supposed vaguely, if only in order to sober herself up. There were eggs and a tin of soup in the kitchen; nothing else. On Wednesdays she was used to a good lunch with Peter. She should have bought something on her way home.

She opened the soup and heated it, and cracked the eggs into a pan to make an omelette. There was some stale bread left, the end of a wholemeal loaf, and she put two slices under the grill to toast; that left only the crust for the next day's breakfast, but tomorrow was still a long way off.

Oh, Peter, she thought, how can I bear it? She looked round her tiny kitchen, her little domain, with all the bits and pieces she had collected so proudly during her working life, and it all seemed meaningless: she knew that none of it, not one of her little comforts or luxuries, was compensation for what she had been denied: a man, an ordinary man, not any special sort, perhaps even rather dull, but kind; and hers.

16

HUGH successfully hid his astonishment when he found Peter Graham sitting, with a whisky and soda, talking to Stella, who was knitting. He had not seen Peter's car, parked outside, for it was round at the front of the house, and he had come in by the back door after putting his own away in the garage. He bent to kiss his wife, and could tell from her response that her day had been eventful.

'Well, Peter.' He raised his hand in salute.

Peter stood up.

'You're late, Hugh. Did you miss the 5.30?'

'Yes, blast it. I had a last-minute panic to cope with,' said Hugh. 'Did you get your shopping done?' He walked over to an old oak corner cupboard where bottles and glasses were kept and poured himself out a drink.

'Yes. Or rather, my secretary did,' said Peter. He looked down at his glass and imagined Joan's face was reflected in it. She seemed to gaze at him reproachfully: no wonder. Then her image faded and he could not conjure it up again. He kept trying, which meant he began to frown and squint, and became inattentive to the conversation. Hugh and Stella exchanged glances across the room.

'You've got a good secretary, haven't you? I've heard you say so.' Hugh wiped the bottom of his glass and came over to the fireplace. He leaned against the mantelpiece and looked at the other two with a benign expression. Peter was sitting down again.

'Yes. She's leaving, though,' he said.

'Oh, bad luck. They often do, just when you've got them trained to your ways. Getting married, I suppose?'

'No, oh no,' said Peter. He wondered what they would say if he told them the truth; they would be sympathetic, he was sure, but he retained enough sense to realise that in the years ahead he might regret the confidence. He might come to resent their knowledge of his secret; and he might find that sharing it would undermine his determination to repair his life. 'I do hate changes,' he said aloud.

'Yes.' Hugh and Stella murmured agreement. They waited to see if he wanted to enlarge upon this statement, and when he said no more Stella judged it time to explain.

'Darling, Peter's had an awful day. His son's had a riding accident and his daughter got married.' She knew that if Hugh was not soon told what had happened he would burst with curiosity.

'Good God! Is the boy all right?' Hugh did not like to comment on the girl.

They told him, in sections, each adding to the other's remarks, about Rupert and about Caroline. Peter left vague the reasons for the hurried secrecy of the wedding, for a latent loyalty to Meriel would not let him reveal the truth.

'Sensible girl,' said Hugh, for the deed was done and why add disapproval to the load of Peter's worries? In any case, after one of each kind, he favoured quiet weddings.

'Nicholas seemed a very nice young man,' said Stella. She was longing to tell Hugh her own views upon the matter; she longed, too, to go to bed. It seemed that Peter would never leave. But he needed them; he needed their company while he strengthened his own resolution, and she knew this. She must be patient.

'Yes, I thought so too.' Peter clutched at this comfort. 'Wish to goodness he wouldn't call me "sir".'

Hugh laughed.

'Poor young devil, he was probably scared stiff of you,' he said. 'I expect he thought you'd want to horsewhip him.'

'Oh, do you think so?' Peter had not previously seen the situation from Nicholas's angle. 'I suppose you're right,' he said. 'Oh well, I'll soothe him down when they get back from Italy, or wherever they've gone. What can I get him to call me? I'm sure he's much too young to get round to my name.'

They spent a few minutes making suggestions, each

most unlikely to solve the problem, with Peter shun-
ning the 'Pa' that Hugh proposed. He had relaxed,
and seemed settled for the evening, until he looked at
his watch and surprised them by leaping to his feet
exclaiming 'Ah!' in a satisfied voice.

'Well, I must be off,' he said. 'Thank you again,
Stella, my dear. I'll be ringing you up. You must come
to dinner next week.'

Still talking, he went out, followed by Hugh who
paused to raise puzzled brows at Stella behind his
back.

'Was he tight? Was it safe to let him drive?' she
asked anxiously as soon as Hugh returned.

'Oh yes. He only had a couple of weak ones,' said
Hugh. 'And it's no distance.'

'He may have had more before he brought me back,
and we all had sherry at the hospital,' said Stella.

Hugh came over to her and sat down on the arm of
her chair. She laid her knitting aside and took his
hand.

'Poor old Peter,' she said meditatively. 'That
Meriel's a bitch.' She began to fill in the gaps for him,
all that could not be said in front of Peter: how
Meriel had insisted still on dining out, and of her refusal to accept Rupert's injury. Even Stella did not
know the whole story. 'Peter came here as a sort of
gesture,' she ended. 'Did you see how he looked at his
watch? He'd decided how long he'd stay, and time
was up.'

'So that's why we're to be asked to dinner,' said Hugh. 'He's going to pick his own friends, is he? The worm has turned, in fact. Splendid!'

'Shall we go? To dinner, I mean,' asked Stella. She leaned against Hugh; he was solid and comforting.

'We won't really be invited. He'll lose his nerve,' said Hugh.

'I'm not so sure,' Stella said. 'I think he meant it. I don't think he'll weaken. Of course, I loathe that woman so much, and she's been so rude to me, cutting me dead hundreds of times, that if it weren't for Peter nothing would make me consider accepting. But it might be rather fun.'

'Oh, I think we'll go if we're asked,' said Hugh. 'We must help old Peter break the shackles.'

'We'd have to invite them back.' Stella's voice was sleepy. 'How could we ever equal their standard of entertaining?' She pondered, while Hugh thought fondly how silly she was to worry about payment in the same coin. As if it mattered. But Stella had solved the problem. 'I know,' she said. 'We'll have them back on Hanni's day off.' She began to giggle, and then had to explain to Hugh that Hanni and Rupert were both likely to become frequent visitors to the house.

'Jolly good,' said Hugh. 'It will keep you from being lonely. Mind you make use of them both. They'll think it a pleasure to work for you.' He kissed her. "Darling, you're almost asleep. You must go to bed. Come on, you've had quite enough for today.'

'Oh, Hugh, I haven't done a thing about supper,' said Stella. 'In fact, I don't think I've even unpacked the shopping. I forgot all about it.'

'Never mind. I'll fix it,' said Hugh. 'Come along, darling.' He pulled her gently to her feet, and she stood smiling at him.

'I am tired,' she admitted. 'But so must you be. Bless you, Hugh. I do love you.'

'That's good. I'm glad,' he said. He held her for a moment, feeling the thickness of her body between them, and a great tenderness for her filled him. He kissed her again. 'Just keep on like that,' he said.

She laughed.

'Oh, Hugh, how silly we are, at our age,' she exclaimed. 'Just look at us.'

'We're not silly,' said Hugh gravely. 'We're lucky. I bet poor old Peter gets mighty few moments like this. Unless—' he stopped.

'Unless what?'

'Oh, nothing.' Hugh had remembered Peter's expression when he talked about his secretary leaving. But this was a thought he would not share with Stella, or anyway, not now.

'Bed, Mrs. Wheeler. Come along,' he said. 'Hurry.'

17

As he drove away from the Wheelers' house, Peter grinned. It was an empty, foolish grin, a mere outward manifestation of his inner revolt. He should not have had that second whisky at old Hugh's. Decent chap, Hugh, and damn' lucky to have Stella; now, there was a woman, a real woman. Must concentrate on driving : it wouldn't do at all if he, a solicitor, was nabbed for drunken driving. Where would his practice be then? And what, oh what, would Meriel say? Carefully, now, no risks, no sudden spurts of acceleration. Mind that bicycle; and here comes the bus, a garish monster like a mobile gin-palace. Round the corner now, in low gear; brake again, and gently between the gateposts; down the drive; and lo, the garage. Damn, the doors are shut. Oh, but here comes Hanni to open them, bless her little Swiss heart.

Still smiling fatuously, Peter sat while Hanni opened the doors for him. He drove in, revved the engine and switched off. Then, with ponderous steps, he went into the house, entering, like Hugh, through the back door.

Hanni was clattering about, nearly ready to dish up.

'Smells good, Hanni,' said Peter. He felt suddenly very hungry.

'It's chicken fricassee, sir,' she said. 'Lots of onion.'

'I'll be ready in a few minutes,' said Peter.

He went into the hall and through to the cloakroom, where he whistled as he washed his hands and brushed his wispy hair. Then, remembering his promise, he went upstairs, walking slowly and holding the banister rail. Rupert's door was ajar, left so by Hanni in case he should call. He lay half on his back, the wounded arm uppermost, abandoned in the sleep of utter exhaustion. Peter watched him for a few minutes; he breathed quietly, never stirring. Peter went quietly away.

Downstairs, the drawing-room door was closed. He wondered if Meriel had gone to bed, reduced to the sulks; but it was unlikely. He thought she would face him and fight.

She was sitting in her usual chair, wearing a dark green dress in which she looked untouchable and elegant. She was studying her part for the play; the book of it lay open in her lap. When he came in, she closed it and reached for her fur wrap which was draped over the arm of the chair.

'So here you are. What have you been doing? I didn't hear the car,' she said. 'We'll be late, I hope they keep the table for us.'

For an instant Peter thought how much easier it would be not to struggle, but simply to comply, as always, with her will. But he resisted the temptation to weakness.

He took a deep breath.

'You didn't hear the car because I put it in the garage,' he said. 'I'm sorry about your birthday dinner, but we'll have it another night. We can't leave Rupert. Hanni is finding something.'

At this point Hanni came in, right on cue, to say that dinner was ready.

Meriel, brought up never to reveal emotion in front of the servants, thanked her, and Peter felt relief. There would be no scene.

'Very well,' said Meriel. 'Since my feelings are not to be considered.' She got up and walked ahead of him into the dining-room.

Excuses rushed to his lips, for the habits of years die hard. But he kept silent, and followed.

Without speaking, Meriel served them both, and they ate, Peter with appetite, but she as though each mouthful were sawdust. Finally she put down her fork and left most of her food untouched on her plate. Peter did not comment; so this was to be the way of it : patient suffering. He did not know that her inability to swallow was genuine; that her obstinate reluctance to give up the planned outing was her way of clinging to what was known, safe and familiar, in the face of Caroline's devastating revelation, and of Peter's own display of independence. She kept her mind closed to what Caroline had said, in case it could be true, and dwelt instead on his conduct in staying down at the Wheelers' house for over an hour; inexcusable at any time, but still more unforgivable on her birthday.

Peter finished his dinner with cheese, while Meriel toyed with some crumbs. Then they returned to the drawing-room where Hanni brought the coffee-tray.

'Rupert sleeps,' she said. 'I will hear if he cries out in the night, so do not worry, Madame.' For form's sake she addressed her remarks to Meriel but she looked at Peter as she spoke.

'Thank you, Hanni. Goodnight.' Once again, habit came to Meriel's rescue as she spoke the customary words. She poured out the coffee with the accustomed movements and handed Peter his cup. He took it from her, put it down on the small table beside him, and lighted his pipe. Then he opened a book. He turned the pages at intervals, but in fact he did not take in a word of what he was reading; he was waiting for the outburst. But it did not seem to be coming.

Meriel had picked up her book of the play again and seemed to be engrossed. He did not know that his own face and Joan's seemed to be staring up at her from the pages, while in her ears echoed Caroline's high, excited voice. She did not think of Rupert, so nearly badly hurt; and she did not think of Caroline's own life and the step she had taken. She thought only of what had happened to herself : now, she allowed the thought, the possibility. The whole structure of her life rocked.

Peter read on. So it was to be a cold war, with no arguing or recriminations, just move and counter-move as he began the campaign to restore his own position and rescue Rupert. He did not expect Meriel to give in without a struggle. She would hold out, regrouping her forces and deploying them in fresh efforts to keep him subjugated; but where it mattered, his resistance would prevail. In the end there might be a truce, an acceptance and a tolerance of each other which would, perhaps, allow the development of something more constructive; but that was for the future.

They sat, their books before them, he with his pipe and she lighting one cigarette after another. At last she stood up, shook the cushions from behind her and emptied the ashtrays into the fire.

'I'm tired, I've had a long day,' she said. 'I'm going up.'

Peter looked at her over his book.

'Very well. I'll see to Pogo tonight,' he said. 'You must begin his training tomorrow. Rupert will help you when he's better. It will give him something to do. Goodnight.'

When she had gone, he laid his book down and stared into the fire. Was this the right way to go on? Or would it be better, more honest, to give it all up and leave? Hugh and Stella had broken away from their separate hells and then had found each other.

But between them there was something special, something that was justification for all that had gone before. He and Joan had no such bond; loneliness, misery, but most of all opportunity, was what had drawn them together. Anyway, the choice was made. He knew he would stay, but no longer acquiesce.

He got up and went over to the box where the puppy lay, still sleeping. Peter picked him up, protesting squeakily at being woken, and took him out into the drive where he put him down and began talking to him encouragingly while he sniffed about. They walked up and down for a while, and then Peter took him back into the house. He tucked him up in his box and carried it out to the kitchen, where it would be warm all night beside the boiler. Pogo would have to learn to sleep there in hygienic solitude. Then he went out into the garden again.

It was damp underfoot, but not cold. Peter walked down the path and to the field at the end. The gate was open, and as he looked across into the darkness a white shape moved with a rustle over the grass. It was Martian, returned. Peter went over to him. The pony stood waiting, docile at last, longing to be relieved of the saddle and bridle which he still wore. The reins were broken, and a stirrup was missing; the saddle was covered in mud where he had rolled, and it had slipped round so that it hung lopsidedly behind his shoulder. Peter undid the girths and took it off; then he slid the bridle over Martian's head. The pony stood meekly, without attempting to bite or kick.

'So you're quelled at last, are you?' said Peter aloud. 'I don't believe it. You'll be back at your tricks to-morrow.' He slapped the animal on his muscular rump, and Martian bucked away, startled. 'I thought so. Well, you're for it, my lad, if anyone will be fool enough to buy you.' Peter sighed at the difficulties; but perhaps in a riding school, pounding away for most of the day, Martian would at last submit. He left the pony to his musings and walked back to the gate, latching it behind him. He carried the filthy, battered saddle and bridle back to the shed where they lived and put them away. Cleaning them would be a day's work, and then they would have to be taken in to Timpsley to the saddler's to be repaired; a nice little job for Meriel. If he went in now she would be asleep, or at least she would have had time to compose herself in an attitude of feigned repose.

Slowly, he mounted the stairs. Tomorrow the task ahead would not seem so arduous.

In his field, Martian, tired after the day's adventures, cropped the grass. Overhead, a few stars patterned the sky. Merelands was a black huddle flanked by trees under the scudding clouds. Two windows showed as lighted squares, breaking the dark mass of the house. Presently one disappeared as Hanni switched off her light, settling down under her blankets with her bedroom door open in case Rupert should call.

182

Peter took longer to be ready, but at last the remaining patch of yellow light vanished. Merelands had finished with the day. Overhead, the sky cleared as the wind blew the last of the storm away. A cat shrieked somewhere in the distance, and a few owls hooted. It would be fine tomorrow.